LOST IN THE
SNOW

LOST IN THE SNOW

by Ben M. Baglio

Interior art by Doris Ettlinger

SCHOLASTIC INC.

New York   Toronto   London   Auckland   Sydney
Mexico City   New Delhi   Hong Kong   Buenos Aires

ISBN-13: 978-0-439-87144-0
ISBN-10: 0-439-87144-1

12 11 10 9 8 7 6 5 4 3 2 1   7 8 9 10 11 12/0

Printed in the U.S.A.
First Scholastic printing, February 2007

Special thanks to Lucy Courtenay

Chapter One

The air was cold and crisp, and Hollow Creek Riding Center's stable yard was thick with densely packed snow that was marked here and there with prints from hooves, tires, and boots. It was winter break and the snow had been on the ground for several weeks. Icicles hung from the stable gutters, and the pond beyond the barn was frozen to a glossy sheen while the Hollow Creek ducks and geese huddled in the shelter of the barn. The forest and high craggy mountains beyond the riding center were also dusted in frosty white, and the pale sun gleamed and twinkled on the icy barn roof.

To Andi Talbot, who had grown up in Florida, snow was one of the most magical things about Orchard Park, the suburb of Seattle, Washington, where she now lived with her mom. She stood for a moment in the middle of the yard and admired the view.

"I hate this weather," Andi's best friend Natalie Lewis grumbled, stamping her feet on the ground as they walked across the yard toward the stables. "My feet are frozen."

"I like it," said Neil O'Connor, walking beside them. Neil's mom ran the riding center. Andi and Natalie had made friends with Neil when they learned to ride a few months ago . . . *and* when they'd helped track down a special horse named Sunshine, who had been snatched right off the center's property.

It was a good thing that Andi, Natalie, and their other best friend, Tristan Saunders, had tons of experience finding animals. After all, they'd started the Pet Finders Club when Andi had lost her dog, Buddy, just after moving to Orchard Park. So it wasn't long before Sunshine was back in the stables safe and sound.

Now, thanks to an arrangement that let them ride the Hollow Creek horses in exchange for helping out at the stables, they saw Neil most weekends.

"Well, it's pretty," Natalie said hastily. She adjusted her thick pink hat over her blond braids. "Just cold."

Mrs. O'Connor came toward them, leading two ponies. "Neil, take Scrumpy, will you?" She passed Neil the shaggy brown pony's halter rope. "Andi, Natalie, would you be able to fetch Bonnie and Bandana? I have a class of four waiting in the sand school, and I'm running late." She nodded her head at the stable block behind her. Two ponies looked over their half-doors and snorted. Their misty breath plumed into the air.

"I'll bring Bonnie," Andi suggested to Natalie, walking over and petting the chestnut pony's nose.

"OK," Natalie said, watching Neil as he walked over to the arena with his mom and the two ponies. "I'll take Bandana." The bay pony with a white blaze on his nose neighed softly at the mention of his name. Still looking at Neil, Natalie unlocked the bottom half of Bandana's stable door and felt around for the pony's halter rope, which was hanging on the stable wall. Bandana snorted crossly as she banged his nose by mistake.

"Oops," said Natalie, stroking the pony's nose. "Sorry, Bandana."

"Good thing your *boyfriend* didn't see that." Andi giggled as she tucked her shoulder-length brown hair into her cap. She liked teasing Natalie about Neil. Her friend had had a crush on him for months but would never admit it.

"He's not my boyfriend!" Natalie said, her blue eyes gleaming. "He's a *friend*."

"Yeah, yeah . . . " Andi towed Bonnie across the stable yard, and Natalie followed with Bandana. They helped Neil and Mrs. O'Connor tack up the ponies and adjust the stirrup lengths for the beginner riders.

Mrs. O'Connor patted Bonnie on the flank. "Thanks for your help," she told the girls. "Now it's time to keep my half of the deal. Why don't you tack up and take a ride yourselves? I was out in the forest first thing this morning. It's gorgeous."

Andi swung around to Neil. "Can we?" she asked eagerly. She looked over her shoulder at the magnificent mountains with their fringe of frosty forest. With a shiver of delight, she thought about riding through those silvery trees.

"Sure," Neil nodded. "Let's go tack up right now."

They followed Neil back across the stable yard to saddle up Flash, Neil's beautiful palomino horse with a pale tan coat and silver mane and tail. Andi chose Chipper, a bright young gelding with an orange-brown coat and a white star-shaped patch between his eyes.

"You take Tilly, Natalie." Neil came out of the tack room with a saddle, which he handed to Natalie. Tilly was a gorgeous red-brown color with a black tail. "Wear these," he added, passing out extra thick gloves and scarves. He then produced a tub of what looked like grease and scooped out a handful.

"Eww." Natalie's face wrinkled as Neil bent down and picked up one of Flash's feet. "What's that for?"

Neil packed the grease deep into Flash's hoof. "It stops the snow from getting into the horses' feet and balling up," he explained. "Horses can go lame in this kind of weather." He did the same thing for Chipper, then Tilly.

Andi laughed when she saw the disgust on Natalie's face. "Just be glad that he didn't ask us to do our own horses," she said as they mounted at last and set off for the forest.

The first stretch of the trail ride followed the side of the cattle paddock, with the river rushing along beside them. Because of the weather, the red-and-white cows were huddled together in the shelter of their stone barn. They watched curiously as Neil led the way, avoiding the deeper snowdrifts and calling warnings over his shoulder about ice.

Soon, the blue sky disappeared and they were beneath the cover of the forest.

"It's like riding through a bunch of Christmas trees," Andi whispered in delight, her chestnut-colored eyes staring up at the outstretched branches of the pines overhead. Her horse, Chipper, walked at a steady pace several yards behind Neil and Natalie, but Andi could hear Natalie's voice echoing in the stillness.

She tried to tune out their conversation. She wanted to listen to the sounds of the forest, not her best friend getting gooey over Neil. She loosened her grip on the reins and stared between the soldier-like tree trunks at the thick white snow, which lay deep in the forest. She could make out animal tracks and even thought she saw a glimpse of a deer before Chipper moved on and the deer disappeared from view. Every now and then, she heard the angry squeak of a squirrel high up in the snowy branches overhead.

Natalie's laughter rang out through the trees. "You tell the best jokes, Neil." There was a sudden shivering in the branches overhead, and a large clump of snow slid off a branch. It landed on Natalie with a thump.

Andi rode Chipper up to join the others, fighting the urge to laugh. "Are you okay, Nat?" she asked, pulling alongside Tilly.

"Fine," Natalie snapped, red with embarrassment as she pushed the snow off her head and shoulders.

Neil grinned. "It's probably not a good idea to laugh out loud in these woods," he advised. "Too much noise shifts the snow."

The horses walked on, down a tunnel of trees. Suddenly, Andi heard something—a crunching of twigs somewhere close by. "Hey!" she whispered to the others. "Did you hear that?"

"What was it?" Natalie said uneasily. She glanced at Neil and steered Tilly closer to Flash.

Andi pulled her horse to a halt and held her breath. There was definitely something moving in the stand of trees just to the left of the track. As she watched, a beautiful snow-white pony stepped out into the light, blowing through quivering nostrils. "Whoa!" Andi said in amazement.

Neil gave a soft whistle as the mare eyed them warily. There was a glint of terror in her eyes as if she recently had been spooked by something. She was about fourteen hands high, Andi decided — around four-and-a-half feet from front hoof to shoulder — and had a pretty dished face with wide-set eyes. While her neatly trimmed mane and tail were a creamy color, her coat was pure white. There was no saddle on her back.

Neil slowly dismounted Flash and carefully footed the snowy incline toward the mare, making soothing noises at her. She snorted and tossed her head, watching him closely, and danced a little to one side as he approached.

Andi crossed her icy fingers tightly in her mittens. She knew that approaching a loose pony, particularly a frightened one, could be very dangerous.

"Hey, beauty," Neil said, keeping his voice soft so as not to alarm the mare. "What are you doing out here all on your own?" The pony neighed at him, shifting nervously from side to side. She flinched as he reached out and stroked her neck.

Andi bit her lip, wondering if the frightened animal was going to bolt, but the mare relaxed after a couple of moments. "She looks very well-bred," Andi murmured, dismounting into a fluff of snow. She studied the mare's profile, which was slightly concave, flaring out at her muzzle. "Don't Arabian horses have dished faces like that?"

Neil nodded, still stroking the mare. "And look how high-set her tail is," he said. "That's another Arabian characteristic." As if to illustrate Neil's point, the mare swished her tail and snorted thick puffs of air through her nostrils.

"She's been taken good care of by someone," Andi went on, noting the mare's sleek coat and well-rounded flanks. She glanced around. There was no one else to be seen. "But by whom?" she added.

"Maybe she bucked off her rider?" Natalie suggested, sliding off Tilly and into a drift.

"What about her saddle?" Andi pointed out. "Do you think she could have lost it?"

Neil moved his hand farther down the mare's neck, until he was stroking her shoulders and her back. He shook his head. "Her coat doesn't look as if it's been flattened by a saddle recently," he said. "She doesn't have a brand mark, either, which could have helped us track down her owner. She's about seven or eight, I'd say—less muscular than an older horse would be, but she's so calm that she must have been handled a lot. Maybe she escaped from a nearby field."

"She's so pretty," Natalie said dreamily, "she could be a unicorn. If she had a horn, I mean."

Andi agreed. There *was* something magical-looking about the mare's glossy white coat and silky mane and the way she had appeared in the middle of the snowy forest. "She's not a unicorn," she said regretfully, "but I'll tell you what she *is*. A beautiful animal, lost in the forest, no sign of a rider . . . she's the latest case for the Pet Finders Club!"

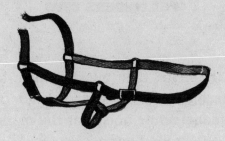

Chapter Two

"We'd better take her back to the riding center," said Neil.

"How are we going to lead her there?" Andi asked. "She's not wearing a bridle."

Neil frowned. Andi checked her saddle, and Natalie did the same, looking for something they might be able to use as a headcollar.

Andi ducked down to check Chipper's girth, and the large metal buckle on her western-style leather belt dug into her belly. Impatiently, she tried to loosen it — and stopped. "Hey!" she said. "How about our belts?"

"Our belts?" Natalie glanced at her pink sparkly belt in dismay. "I only bought this last week."

"You'll get it back." Andi held out her hand to Natalie and raised her eyebrows. Natalie glanced at Neil, who was already unbuckling his belt. With a sigh, she did the same and handed it over.

Neil took the belts, then buckled them together and twisted them into a rough sort of headcollar. Pursing his lips, he made gentle noises at the mare and slowly looped the belts around her neck.

"I knew it would work," said Andi triumphantly.

Neil mounted his horse, holding the makeshift lead-rein in one hand. Then they set off, following Neil and the mare back through the trees, down beside the river, and back to Hollow Creek.

In the yard, the beginners' lesson had finished. Still holding the mare, Neil rode Flash over to where his mom was standing. Andi slid off Chipper's back and tethered him to a nearby rail. Then she hurried to join Neil, who was deep in conversation with his mom. Natalie followed.

"Did Neil tell you how we found her in the forest?" Andi asked breathlessly. "I thought I was imagining things when she stepped out of the trees! It was like something out of a fairy tale."

"She's a beauty, all right," Mrs. O'Connor said as she stroked the mare's nose. "Are you sure there was no rider with her?"

"We didn't see anyone," Andi said, putting her hand on the pony's flank. "And Neil didn't think her hair looked like it had been flattened by a saddle."

Mrs. O'Connor ran her hand gently around the mare's belly. "You're right," she said after a moment. "The hair here, around her girth, would show the marks of a saddle most clearly, and there's nothing." She straightened up and looked thoughtfully at the pony. "So what are we going to do with her?" she asked.

Neil glanced at Andi and Natalie. "We were kind of hoping to put her up here for a while, Mom," he said. "Just until we find her owner."

Mrs. O'Connor looked concerned. "Here?" she said.

"Is that a problem, Mrs. O'Connor?" Andi asked, stroking the mare's neck.

"I'm afraid so," Mrs. O'Connor said. "You see, we've only got one free stable at the moment—and we have a paying guest arriving next weekend—Puffin. He's a four-year-old gelding whose owner, Mr. Forster, is remodeling his stables."

"I'm sure we'll be able to find the mare's owner by next weekend," said Andi, trying to sound more confident than she felt.

Mrs. O'Connor seemed doubtful. "If you say so," she said. "Mr. Forster's paid two weeks' livery costs in advance. If you still haven't found this beauty's owner by Saturday, I'm afraid you'll have to find other accommodations for her."

"We will," Andi promised. "Do you know anyone who might have lost a mare, Mrs. O'Connor?"

"No one comes to mind," Mrs. O'Connor replied. "I'll make a few calls to see if anyone's missing a gray while you unhitch your ponies."

"Um, Mrs. O'Connor?" Natalie said. "The pony's white, not gray."

"That's the equine term for ponies with pure white coats," Neil explained, leading the mare toward an empty stable at the end of the block. "Gray."

"Oh." Natalie blushed. "Right."

"We'll help you groom and stable the mare in a minute, Mrs. O'Connor," Andi promised. She ran to untie Chipper from the fence post and lead him back to his stable. Lifting off his saddle, she laid it down gently on the straw-covered ground and took up a body brush. She groomed Chipper until his sorrel coat shone, then rugged him up and put some fresh hay in his feed rack. Last of all, she returned Chipper's saddle to the tack room.

Neil put his head over Tilly's stable door as Andi and Natalie were stuffing hay into Tilly's feed rack. "Yours, I believe," he said, holding up a handful of belts.

"Thanks." Natalie reached for her pink belt, and Andi took hers. When they were finished with Tilly, the girls headed to the gray mare's stable and peered over the door.

Mrs. O'Connor was brushing the mare's snowy coat. There was fresh hay in the feed rack, and the pony was munching contentedly. Andi hadn't touched the pony in the forest because she hadn't wanted to spook her. Suddenly, she wondered what her smooth white coat felt like. Would it be as silky as it looked?

"I'll do that if you like, Mrs. O'Connor," she offered, holding out her hand for the body brush.

"Thanks, Andi." Mrs. O'Connor gave it to her. "I'll make a start on those phone calls. Neil, go see if you can find a spare rug for her. I'm sure we've got a couple on the shelf in the tack room."

"I'll help you, Neil!" Natalie hurried after him, and Mrs. O'Connor headed for the office. Andi was left on her own with the mare.

"It's just you and me, then," she said softly, reaching out a tentative hand and resting it on the mare's neck. The pony tossed her head watchfully but didn't flinch away. Her coat felt warm and soft beneath Andi's fingers. Gently, Andi worked the brush down the pony's back, brushing in even strokes. As she groomed the pony's shoulders, she noticed an old scar, marked by a ridge of hair that grew the wrong way. It was narrow and curved

but had healed well. Bending down to brush the pony's legs, she felt warm breath blowing down her neck.

"I guess this must be pretty weird, huh," Andi said, straightening up and running her fingers along the mare's pricked ears. The mare snorted at her. "Don't worry. We'll find your owner soon—I promise." She glanced at the weather and shivered. If they didn't find the mare's owner by the weekend, what were they going to do? Somehow, she couldn't imagine her mom letting her tether a pony in the backyard.

"We found a rug for her!" Natalie handed the dark blue material over the stable door. "Come on, I want to know if Mrs. O'Connor's located the pony's owner yet."

Andi buckled the rug onto the gray mare's back, making sure she was warm and snug. The pony pricked her ears and made a soft, whickering noise through her nostrils. Then Andi bolted the stable door behind her and followed Natalie across the yard to the office.

Mrs. O'Connor motioned them inside. "Are you absolutely sure?" she said, cradling the phone with her shoulder as she jotted something down. "About fourteen hands, Arabian blood? Right—okay—thanks."

"Good news?" Andi said hopefully.

Mrs. O'Connor shook her head. "I've called the two closest ranches," she said with a frown. "No one's missing a gray. It's a real mystery what that mare was doing out in the forest all on her own."

"Did you ask if they had any spare stables we could use for her if we don't find her owner by the weekend?" Andi asked.

Mrs. O'Connor nodded. "They do, but livery costs are expensive." She named a price for food and stabling that made Andi wince.

"Now what?" Neil asked.

"Time for the Pet Finders to start work, I think," said Andi, tearing her thoughts away from the worry of stabling the mare. "Follow me, guys. We've got a lot to do."

An hour later, Andi stood up from examining the base of a pine tree in the clearing where they had found the pony. They had walked back into the forest, hoping to find some clues about how the pony came to be wandering loose under the trees.

"Find anything?" Natalie called from the other side of the clearing.

"Not unless you count the toes that just dropped off my feet." Andi sighed. So far, they'd checked out everything in a twenty-yard circle of where they found the pony and come up with absolutely nothing. And in spite of her gloves, extra socks, and wool hat, Andi was starting to feel as if she was turning blue with cold.

"I got a weird-looking stone," Natalie offered, holding something up for Andi to see.

Neil looked over Natalie's shoulder. "That's not a rock, Nat. It's frozen horse dung."

Natalie shrieked and dropped it like a hot potato. Andi and Neil laughed.

"Let's widen the search," Andi said when she'd recovered. Slowly they widened the circle: thirty yards, then forty. The trees were getting thicker, and the snow teetered in piles on the undisturbed branches. Remembering what had happened to Natalie earlier, Andi took care to shake the snow away from any overhanging branches that were too close for comfort. The snow lay in drifts and piles. Strange bumps just beneath the surface turned out to be fallen branches or pine cones.

Andi's back was starting to ache. She pushed through what felt like her thousandth heap of snow—and her fingers touched something cold and hard. Pulling out her find, she examined it curiously. It was made from stiff blue fabric, with a metal ring and a rope hooked on to one side—it looked familiar, but it hung from her fingers as if it had somehow been busted open.

It's a headcollar, she realized and swung around in

excitement. "I've got a clue!" she shouted. "Over here, quick!"

Neil and Natalie ran across the clearing.

"Just what we've been looking for!" Neil took the head-collar from Andi's hands and examined it.

"It's broken, see?" Andi pointed to where the strong webbing had torn roughly in two. Then she pointed at a clump of white hair that was caught in the metal ring with a fresh surge of excitement. "White hair! It *has* to belong to the mare!"

"This makes it less likely that the pony escaped from a field," Neil murmured, still turning the headcollar around in his hands. "We never let our horses out with their headcollars on. They might catch it on a fence or shrub and hurt themselves."

"But we keep the headcollar underneath the bridle when we take a horse out for a ride," Natalie pointed out. "That way we can tether the horse if we take off the bridle. Maybe someone was riding her this morning after all."

"There's still the problem of there being no saddle marks," Neil pointed out. "And where's the bridle?"

Natalie's face fell.

"And you'd expect to see scratches and bruises on

a horse that ran away from its rider," Neil added. "She didn't seem hurt when we found her."

Andi thought of the jagged mark she'd seen when she was grooming the pony. "I saw a scar on her withers when I was brushing her," she said, "but it looked like it had been there a while. There weren't any new marks, but she had been spooked by something when we found her, hadn't she?"

Neil and Natalie both nodded. The mare had certainly been jumpy about something.

"Let's take the headcollar back to the center, Neil," Andi suggested. "Your mom might have heard something from the police by now."

"Yes, let's go," Natalie said in relief. "It's freezing out here."

Pumped up from the excitement of their find, Andi felt a rush of energy as they headed back to the riding center. She bounced up and down a couple of times then broke into a run, drinking in the fierce, cold air that filled her lungs.

Bounding into the stable yard, full of ideas about the clues they'd found, Andi stopped short at the sight of her mom's car. Mrs. Talbot was talking to Neil's mom, huddled in a sheltered spot by the office.

"Right on time, Andi!" Judy Talbot smiled. "Is Natalie with you?"

"Do we have to go *now*?" Andi asked with dismay. She'd totally forgotten that her mom was coming to pick her up at one. "We just found a fantastic clue about a missing pony, and we just *have* to follow it up! Mrs. O'Connor, we found a broken headcollar—Nat and Neil are just behind me with it. We—"

"Sorry, Andi, but we have to go," her mom interrupted gently. "Maybe you can come back tomorrow." Mrs. O'Connor nodded in agreement.

Natalie and Neil clattered into the yard, the broken headcollar slung over Neil's arm. Andi gazed at them, itching to run over and take another look at their precious clue.

"Tomorrow's okay, I guess," she muttered. Then her eyes widened. "Oh, no! Tomorrow's the grand opening of the new Rain Forest Exhibition at the Science Museum. Tristan's so excited about it—there are going to be snakes there, and you know how he feels about *them*. Nat and I promised we'd go with him!"

Tristan Saunders was Andi's other best friend and the third member of the Pet Finders Club. He worked part-time at the local pet store, Paws for Thought, and was crazy about reptiles of any kind.

"Ugh," Natalie groaned as she joined Andi beside the Talbots' car. "Snakes? No thank you! I can't *believe* we let Tristan talk us into it."

"I heard about that exhibition," said Neil. "It sounds pretty cool."

"Hey!" Natalie exclaimed. "Maybe you could come with us, Neil. I wouldn't be so afraid of the snakes if you were there."

Andi dug Natalie in the ribs. Did she have to be so *obvious*?

"Sorry, but I promised Mom I'd help out in the yard tomorrow," Neil said regretfully.

Natalie turned to Andi. "Maybe we can put Tristan off until Monday," she said. "I'd really like to come back to the stables tomorrow. What if someone comes to claim the gray mare and we miss out?"

Neil had turned away to speak to his mom, showing her the broken headcollar.

"What if some girl turns up and steals Neil from under your nose, you mean," Andi teased Natalie quietly, making her blush. "I know it's tough, Nat," she said in a louder voice. "I want to know what happens to the pony, too. But we promised Tristan, and we can't let him down."

"Don't worry, Andi," said Mrs. O'Connor. "Neil and I will keep you posted."

After thanking Mrs. O'Connor and saying good-bye to Neil, Andi and Natalie reluctantly climbed into the car.

"Mrs. O'Connor told me all about the gray pony." Mrs. Talbot pulled out of the Hollow Creek Riding Center's driveway, heading back to Orchard Park. "Sounds pretty exciting."

"It is." Andi sighed. Suddenly, attending Tristan's exhibition tomorrow seemed like a really bad idea. What if Natalie was right and someone did come and claim the mare tomorrow? They wouldn't get to say good-bye.

"These things take time," Mrs. Talbot said gently, as if she could tell what Andi was thinking. "When have any of your cases gotten cleared up in just a day?"

Unconvinced, Andi stared out of the window at the darkening sky. It looked like there was going to be more snow. Through her gloom, she felt glad that the beautiful gray mare would be safe and warm in a Hollow Creek stable tonight. Maybe her mom was right. Maybe they would get to say good-bye after all.

Chapter Three

Andi woke the next morning to see bright snowy light spilling through a gap in her pale blue curtains. A little tan-and-white terrier bounced into her bedroom as her mom opened the door.

"Buddy!" Andi opened her arms and the terrier bounded onto her bed with a bark of delight. She cuddled his warm little body close as he tried to cover her face with licks. "Sorry I didn't spend much time with you yesterday," she said, dropping a kiss on his rough brown nose. "I'll make up for it soon, okay?"

"Tristan just called," Mrs. Talbot said, drawing back the drapes. "He, Natalie, Christine, and Fisher are coming to pick you up around nine for the exhibition." Christine Wilson ran Paws for Thought and was Tristan's mom's cousin, while Fisher Pearce was the local vet and a good friend of Christine's and the Pet Finders Club.

"What time is it?" Andi asked, squinting in the

daylight. More snow lay around the yards and streets outside the window, and the tops of the distant mountains stood like icebergs on the horizon. The light was so bright that it could have been midday.

"Eight-fifteen." Her mom gave Andi a kiss and ruffled her hair. "Just enough time to have breakfast and take Buddy for a stroll around the block."

As soon as he heard his name, Buddy renewed his attempts to lick Andi's face. Laughing, Andi pushed him away. "Eww, dog breath!" she joked. "I'll be down in ten minutes, Mom."

After dressing, Andi ran downstairs and gulped down a bowl of cereal and some juice. "Come on, Bud," she called, pulling on her thickest coat and waving Buddy's leash. "Time for your walk!"

There was never much traffic on Aspen Drive on a Sunday morning, and everything looked plump and perfect beneath its fresh covering of snow. Andi kicked through the drifts, thinking of the gray pony they'd found yesterday as Buddy skipped and danced beside her. How could a gorgeous, well-cared-for pony like that get lost and nobody come to claim it?

Rounding the corner of Aspen Drive again, Andi saw that Fisher's SUV had just pulled up outside her house. "Great day for a nice museum trip!" Fisher smiled at

Andi from the driver's seat, and Christine waved at her from over Fisher's shoulder.

Tristan peered out of the back window. His freckled face was flushed with excitement and his red hair was sticking up even more than usual. "Hey! Hurry up and get your stuff. We want to get to the front of the line!"

"Like the snakes can't wait," Natalie muttered from where she was sitting beside Tristan. Andi guessed that Tristan's enthusiasm had already worn her down.

Andi dropped Buddy inside the house and kissed her mom. Then she scrambled into the backseat with her two friends. "Did you tell Tris about the pony?" she asked as Fisher pulled away from the curb.

Natalie nodded, looking more cheerful. "I called the riding center this morning to see if Neil had any news."

"Ooh, *Neil*." Tristan clutched his heart and looked dramatic. Natalie gave him a scornful look.

"And did he?" Andi prompted.

"Oh, yes," said Tristan. "He told Natalie that he couldn't live without her and—*ouch*! That hurt!" He rubbed his arm where Natalie had smacked him.

"As I was saying." Natalie pushed her blond hair behind her ears and deliberately turned her back on Tristan. "Neil told me that nobody reported a missing pony to the police. He had no luck with the headcollar, either. There's no label or name on it or anything like that. Mrs. O'Connor is going to get it fixed sometime soon so it can be picked up with the mare when we find her owner."

Andi was disappointed that their big clue wasn't much help. "Is the pony okay?" she asked anxiously.

"Yup. Eating everything they give her," Natalie said. "So that's good."

"Until Saturday at least." Andi sighed.

"What's happening on Saturday?" Fisher asked over his shoulder.

Andi explained the stabling problem. "Hey!" she gasped, struck by an idea. "Couldn't the ASPCA take her in that weekend, Fisher?"

Fisher shook his head. "We don't have the resources for such a large animal in Orchard Park. I'll check out some horse adoption agencies for you, though, if you like."

"But what if the owner's looking for her?" Andi said. "We can't give the mare to an adoption agency until we know for sure what's going on."

Pondering the problem, Andi, Tristan, and Natalie hardly noticed as the SUV turned off the road and up the driveway of the Science Museum. There was already a small line of people forming outside the great double doors, waiting patiently for the place to open.

As soon as Fisher had parked, Tristan scrambled out. He raced at a patch of ice and skidded down the line, swerving neatly so he landed at the back. Andi and Natalie followed more slowly, with Fisher and Christine bringing up the rear.

"Did you know," Tristan said, his eyes gleaming as he clapped his hands and stamped his feet to keep warm, "that the longest boa constrictor ever recorded was *forty-nine feet long*?"

"Not true." A boy two places ahead stared earnestly at them. He looked younger than Andi and her friends and wore glasses that sat a little off-balance on his nose. "That's not true," he said again, sounding smug. "When journalists went to check out the claim, it turned out that the snake was only twenty-one feet long."

"*Hello?*" Tristan growled. "This is a private conversation, you know."

"I read it in the latest issue of *Reptiles Today*," the boy continued. "Didn't you?"

Tristan opened his mouth and then closed it again.

"What's the matter, Tristan?" Andi asked sympathetically as the boy in front turned around and the line began to move. "Haven't you read that issue yet?"

Natalie giggled.

"Who asked him, anyway?" Tristan muttered. He glared at the other boy's back as they shuffled forward, heading for the great double doors of the Science Museum.

Andi was relieved to move from the bitter cold outside to the warmth within the museum. The ceiling was lofty and arched high above them, and terrariums were placed at intervals around the large, well-lit room. Andi looked around, unsure where to start.

"Does everything here *crawl*?" Natalie asked in horror, staring at the display cases of insects and lizards, frogs and spiders. "There must be a few cute rain-forest creatures, too. What about monkeys?"

"Guys!" Tristan came running toward them. "I found the snake habitat section down here. It's totally awesome!"

Andi and Natalie followed Tristan, who sped up to get ahead of the crowd. Andi had to admit that he was right to be impressed. The snake habitat was enormous, taking up an entire room in the museum. There was just enough space around and above the glass cases for visitors to see the snakes from every possible angle. There were Amazonian vines and tree stumps, a stagnant-looking pond in one enclosure, and a real, flowing stream with a bubbling cascade at the other. Labels were stuck around the enclosures, giving details on the various snakes that lay coiled along branches or sleeping beneath heat lamps.

"You owe us big time, Tris," Natalie muttered, staying as far away from the habitats as she could while Tristan ran from case to case, pointing out reptiles.

"The anaconda is okay." Tristan waved at a display case containing the most enormous snake Andi had ever seen. "But Emerald, the boa constrictor, is the best." He came to a triumphant halt beside a large, central enclosure made to look like a Brazilian rain forest, with plants and rocks jumbled together.

Emerald lay on one of the rocks, close to a heat lamp, which hung a little way overhead. Her long, pale tan coils were marked with exquisite red and brown patterns, and her head was slender and faintly dog-like, Andi decided—the skull a little larger than the jaws. She looked around eight feet long.

"They train boas in South America to catch mice and rats in their houses," Tristan said, gazing dreamily at Emerald. "Much cooler than having a cat."

Although Andi didn't like snakes much—they were too cold and clammy for her taste—she agreed that Emerald was a fascinating animal. Still, she was glad that thick glass was between her and the boa constrictor.

"A full-grown boa can crush a grown man's rib cage," said Tristan cheerfully.

"Has a boa constrictor ever eaten a person?" Andi asked, not sure she wanted an answer.

Tristan was about to reply when a familiar voice butted in.

"Oh, yes," said the boy they'd seen in line outside. He was standing next to Emerald's enclosure, polishing his glasses with the bottom of his shirt. "The earliest record of a boa eating a human dates back to 1913. I expect they were doing it for years before that, too—it's just no one recorded stuff like that back then."

"Thanks," Andi began.

"I knew that," Tristan said quickly.

"Did you?" Putting his glasses back on, the boy studied Tristan. "My name's Simon. I have a corn snake named Pedro. He's about three feet long."

"Wow, almost as tall as you," said Tristan, sounding sarcastic. "That's nothing. I work with corn snakes every weekend that could eat your corn snake for dinner."

Simon rolled his eyes and sighed. "Corn snakes don't eat each other," he said with a serious expression on his face. "They prefer mice."

"Whatever," Tristan replied. He turned to Andi. "Come

on. Let's go see the eyelash vipers. They're *totally* deadly."

Andi fought the urge to laugh. "Looks like Tristan's met his match," she whispered to Natalie, who grinned.

"Wait. You work with snakes?" Simon asked, staring at Tristan as if he didn't quite believe him. "What's your name?"

"Work with them . . . *rescue* them . . . whatever," Tristan said, leaning nonchalantly against an enclosure. "I found a whole lot of missing snakes once. I'm Tristan."

Andi was about to step in and remind Tristan that he hadn't exactly found the snakes on his own—the Pet Finders Club had all worked to track them down after Paws for Thought had been broken into—when a tall blond-haired man with a neatly trimmed beard stepped up to them. His nametag read: ANDREW COOMBS, HANDLER.

"Are you kids enjoying the exhibition?" he asked.

Andi and the others nodded.

"I thought I heard the voices of some real snake lovers over here." Andrew Coombs smiled at Simon then turned to Tristan. "Did I hear you say you once rescued some reptiles?"

Andi frowned at Tristan, sending strong thought waves in his direction. *Don't you dare take all the credit!*

"My friends and I have a Pet Finders Club," Tristan

said, sounding a little reluctant to share the limelight. "We found about thirty missing reptiles once. Including," he added casually, glancing at Simon, "a Californian king snake and a python."

"A python?" said Simon. "I got real close to a rattler in Arizona one time."

Tristan bristled.

"You kids really do love snakes, huh?" said Andrew Coombs. "Well, you should all come back some day when it's a little quieter in here. You could give me a hand feeding the snakes and cleaning out the cages . . . if it's okay with your folks."

"Count me out," said Natalie, with real feeling.

"No disrespect, Mr. Coombs," Andi added hurriedly, not wanting to appear rude. "It's just..."

"Snakes aren't your thing?" Andrew Coombs nodded. "Fair enough. How about you boys?"

Tristan looked like someone had pressed an enormous Christmas gift into his hands. "Are you serious?"

"Thank you, Mr. Coombs," said Simon. "I've read about the feeding habits of most rainforest snakes. It would be awesome to feed them for real."

"I don't think Tristan likes the competition much," Andi whispered to Natalie, as Tristan shot another sour glance at the younger boy.

"Serves him right," Natalie said, tossing her head. "He was being so mean to me in the car about Neil."

Andi glanced at the coiling, hissing creatures around them. Finding those reptiles for Paws for Thought was one thing—the bigger snakes had been in cages and none of them had been poisonous. But imagine one of these rain-forest reptiles getting loose—like the deadly eyelash viper Tristan had mentioned—and crawling around Orchard Park for them to find . . . that was one case Andi didn't like the sound of!

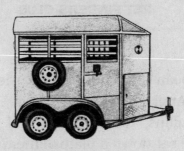

Chapter Four

"Hot ginger tea." Fisher set down five steaming mugs on one of the tables at the Banana Beach Café. "Just the stuff to pep you up on a cold day."

Andi sniffed at her mug. It smelled spicy and a little unusual. "If you say so," she replied, taking a sip. It was delicious! Kind of like gingerbread, but extra warming.

They'd left the Science Museum about an hour earlier and come straight to Jango and Maggie Pearce's Banana Beach Café, back in Orchard Park. Andi practically had to drag Tristan away from a cage containing gaboon vipers—brownish-yellow snakes that hid in the leaves on the rain forest floor and could kill with one bite. It was superwarm in the café, so much that they could all peel off their extra layers of clothes and enjoy the snowy scene outside. Jango and Maggie, Fisher's parents, and owners of the café, liked it warm. They were more used to the Caribbean sun than the Seattle snow. Coming from Florida, Andi knew how they felt.

"Banana muffins, too," Tristan said approvingly, as Maggie Pearce set down a plate of them in the middle of the table. "Great idea, coming here after the exhibition, Fisher. It feels like we haven't left the rain forest yet!"

"Let's hope there are no anacondas under the table," said Natalie with a nervous laugh.

"Have you checked your cell to see if Neil left a message about the pony?" Andi asked, nodding at Natalie's fluffy pink purse.

"About twenty times," Natalie admitted. "I wish we could speak to him. Do you want to go back there tomorrow?"

"Sure," Andi nodded. "We've got to solve this case by Saturday, or the gray mare is in big trouble."

"Count me in," said Tristan, polishing off his muffin in record time.

"Do you need any help, Mrs. Pearce?" Andi offered, putting down her mug as Fisher's mom pulled out a cleaning cloth and started wiping down the café tables.

Maggie Pearce smiled at her. "I need to clean out Long John Silver's cage, since you ask," she said. The blue and green parrot sitting by the bar clicked his beak at the mention of his name. "The clean newspaper is in the back," Maggie continued. "Could you grab me some?"

Andi headed behind the counter and out to the storeroom. A pile of newspapers was stacked neatly by the back door. She picked up the top one and glanced casually at the front page as she carried it back through to the eating area.

"Hey!" She stopped dead and stared at one of the headlines: TRAILER ACCIDENT: PONY MISSING. She read the article as fast as she could.

"Guys!" Andi hurried over to the table, waving the newspaper. "Listen to this! '*An auction truck and trailer carrying three ponies crashed yesterday afternoon on Pines Road. The driver was unhurt, but the trailer wasn't hitched correctly and the ponies escaped. Two were later recovered. The third is still missing. The ponies, part of the estate of the late Mrs. Diana Osmond, were on their way to auction when the accident took place. It is thought to have been caused by icy driving conditions.*' " She looked up. "Where's Pines Road?"

Natalie's eyes were sparkling with excitement. "Really close to the forest where we found the mare!"

"So our gray mare must be the missing pony!" Andi said triumphantly.

Tristan took the paper. "This is yesterday's edition," he said, examining the article. "What does *estate* mean, anyway?"

"When someone dies, their possessions are known as their estate," Fisher explained. "They're often given away or sold at auction if there's nobody to take them. This Diana Osmond must have had a stable."

"But what about her family?" Andi objected. "Surely they wanted the ponies?"

Christine shook her head. "Not necessarily," she said. "Ponies are a lot of work. Maybe Mrs. Osmond's family lives in the city, or maybe they need the money."

"Or maybe she has no family at all," Fisher added.

"That's awful," Andi said, sitting down at the table. She knew that the old lady must have loved her ponies greatly. You could tell just by looking at how well the mare had been taken care of.

"I know what you mean," Tristan said. "But there's another way of looking at this, Andi. This is a totally awesome clue!"

Natalie pulled out her cell phone and dialed the riding center's number, pressing the speakerphone button so everyone could hear the conversation. "Neil?" she said after a moment. "It's Natalie. We think we have some news about the pony!"

Andi peered over Natalie's shoulder as Natalie's read the article to him over the phone. Tristan swiped the last muffin and shuffled closer so he could hear the conversation.

"I'll get Mom to call the auction house right away," Neil said when Natalie had finished the article. "Why don't you all come over tomorrow? Perdita would love to see you."

"Who's Perdita?" Natalie asked, looking as confused as Andi felt.

Neil laughed. "That's what we named the pony. It means 'lost one' in Latin. Cool, huh? See you tomorrow!"

The following morning was cold and gray. Andi wound her warmest scarf around her neck and tucked it into the collar of her coat. Buddy jumped around her feet, his stumpy brown tail wagging excitedly. Andi's mom was working today, so Natalie's mom was giving them a lift to the riding center.

A horn beeped from outside.

"Sorry, Bud," Andi said, hunkering down to give him a hug. "I'd really love to take you, but you know what it's like at the stables. All those big horse feet, just waiting to step on you."

Buddy stopped jumping and lay down. He whined and

looked at Andi with enormous, sad brown eyes. Andi felt awful as she dropped a kiss on the top of his head and hurried out of the door.

In the back of Mrs. Peters' car, Andi sat with her feet as close to the heating vent as she could get them. If anything, it was even colder than yesterday.

"Does my hair look okay?" Natalie asked, tying back her blond locks with a red velvet band as her mom pulled into the Hollow Creek driveway.

"It's hair," Andi sighed, puffing her own brown fringe out of her eyes. "What look were you going for, exactly?"

The girls got out and found Tristan and Neil waiting for them in the yard.

"I don't have good news," Neil said. "Mom called the auction house first thing this morning. They said they couldn't help and told us to talk to the pony's owner."

"But Mrs. Osmond's dead," Natalie pointed out.

"Exactly," Neil said. "And she doesn't have any family, either. Her lawyers are dealing with her estate and selling her stuff. Mrs. Osmond wanted all the money to go to the International League for the Protection of Horses."

"Can't we contact her lawyers?" Tristan asked.

Neil shrugged. "I tried, but the receptionist at the auction house kept putting me on hold. Then told me she couldn't find a name or a number for them."

"What about Mrs. Osmond's house and stable yard?"

"Mom and I drove over there first thing," Neil explained. "The yard was locked up, so we couldn't go in and take a look."

Andi was overwhelmed with frustration. "This is weird!" she said. "Doesn't anyone care about this pony?"

"I guess not," Neil said grimly. "But Perdita's so beautiful—I can't imagine how anyone wouldn't care about her."

Andi sighed. Sometimes it was hard to understand grown-ups. "How is Perdita, anyway?" she asked, glancing along the row of stable doors in search of the mare's snowy coat.

Neil's smile lit up his face. "Come and see for yourself."

"Neil is so cool, right?" Natalie whispered to Tristan as they followed the older boy down the block of stables.

"You've liked stranger people," Tristan replied, which Andi guessed was a compliment.

Perdita whickered her pleasure as Andi and Natalie

scrambled to stroke her nose. Tristan stood with his hands in his pockets, watching Neil fill Perdita's feed rack.

"Isn't she awesome?" Andi asked Tristan.

"Cute," Tristan said. "For a horse."

"How can you like *snakes* better than *horses*?" Natalie asked, rubbing Perdita under her chin. "She's the best!"

"Hey, maybe we should go to the auction house ourselves?" Tristan suggested, turning to Neil. "We could ask the receptionist face-to-face about Mrs. Osmond's lawyers. Maybe she'd help if we pressed her harder. Plus, the driver of that trailer worked for the auction house, didn't he?"

"We could ask him if he remembers a gray!" Andi exclaimed, leaning her face closer to Perdita's elegant nose and feeling the pony's warm breath on her cheek. "Great idea, Tris."

They gave Perdita one last stroke and followed Neil to the office. Mrs. O'Connor was standing by a filing cabinet with a stack of papers in her hand. She greeted them with a warm smile.

"Mom, is there any chance you could give us a ride to the auction house?" Neil asked. "Tristan suggested talking to a few people who worked there."

"I've got a pretty busy morning," Mrs. O'Connor began, staring down at her papers.

"Come on. You don't *really* want to do that filing." Neil took the papers from his mother and put them down on the desk. "Don't you have any errands that might take you near the auction house? It's close to town."

Mrs. O'Connor laughed. "I guess I do have to go get that waterproof rug mended," she said. "Okay. Give me five minutes and I'll take you over there."

Twenty minutes later, Mrs. O'Connor swung into the drive of McVitie's Auction Rooms and parked outside the main office.

"I've got to pop over to Malley's for the rug," she said as Andi and the others got out. "I'll come back around eleven-thirty, okay?"

The auction house reception area was stuffy and messy, piled high with papers and files. The receptionist looked like she was in her twenties, with blond hair piled high on her head and enormous earrings that swung down almost to her shoulders. She was stabbing hopelessly at the computer buttons in front of her.

"Excuse me?" Andi ventured.

The girl looked up hopefully. "Do you know anything about computers?"

"I do." Tristan stepped forward. "What's the problem?"

The girl sighed. "I don't know what the problem is," she said. "*That's* the problem."

"We're here about a missing pony," Andi said. "We wondered if you could answer a couple of questions for us?"

"Did you call this morning?" the girl asked. "I told you I couldn't help. I haven't been able to help *anyone* today. The computer's down again and I don't know where anything is. Look at this place!" She waved at the teetering stacks of paper. "The agency didn't say anything about what a mess it was when they called me in for the job!" She stabbed at another computer button. "'*It's a simple job, Stacey,*'" she mimicked, in what was clearly supposed to be the voice of her recruiter.

"So you're just filling in here?" asked Andi.

"Thank goodness," the girl muttered. "The full-time receptionist will be back on Monday. Poor guy." She hit two computer buttons at once. The computer bleeped miserably, but the screen stayed frozen in place.

Andi glanced at the others. This was hopeless. They were never going to get the name and number of Mrs. Osmond's lawyers this way. "Okay," she said at last, "could you maybe help us with something else? We need to talk to the driver who was involved in the accident the other day."

"What accident?"

"There was an accident with a trailer containing three ponies on the weekend," Natalie said.

"I only started today," said the girl. "Sorry. You'd better ask around the yard. Or you could wait until the full-time guy gets back from vacation."

"You said Monday, right?" Andi shook her head. That was too late for the stabling problem.

"Uh-huh." The girl sat down suddenly in her chair, looking exhausted. "Listen, kid, no offense, but I'm kind of busy here. This job may only pay ten bucks an hour, but it's better than nothing."

As if it was listening, the phone on the desk suddenly rang. The girl snatched it up. "McVitie's Auction House, how may I help you?"

"Well, that was useful," Natalie said sarcastically as they stepped back outside into the biting cold.

"Monday's too long for us to wait," Andi said, frustrated as she thought about the gelding that would kick Perdita out of her place in the stable. "We have to find her owner before then."

She stared around the yard and spotted a short man

with scuffed-up cowboy boots who was hosing down a trailer next to the auction ring. "Excuse me?" she called, hurrying over. "We're looking for the driver of the truck that had the accident on Pines Road over the weekend. Can you help us?"

The guy kept hosing the trailer. "That would be Tom," he said. "He's on vacation this week."

"What? Is everybody on vacation in this place?" Tristan whispered into Andi's ear.

Andi shrugged. "It's winter break," she suggested. "Mom always takes a few days off when I'm home from school."

"Do you know when Tom's back from his vacation?" Natalie asked.

"Friday." The guy turned off the faucet and coiled the hose at his feet. "Have you tried Eddie?"

Andi perked up. "Who's Eddie?"

"He was in the truck with Tom," the man said. "We always work in pairs. You'll find Eddie in the ring."

"The ring" turned out to be the livestock auction room—a high-ceilinged barn with a scattering of sawdust on the ground in the middle of a circle of wooden benches in tiers. A thin kid with a gold earring in his left ear was sweeping halfheartedly at the sawdust.

"Are you Eddie?" Andi asked hopefully.

The boy stopped sweeping and glanced at them. "Who wants to know?"

Andi introduced herself and the others. "We heard you were involved in the trailer accident the other day. Is that right?"

"Yup." The boy started sweeping again. "Lucky not to have my neck broken. Tom hit a piece of ice like you've never seen. I thought the whole truck was going to flip."

"Did you load the ponies into the trailer?" Natalie asked.

The boy shrugged. "Tom did most of it. There's a trick to it that I don't really get."

"Do you remember if you were carrying a gray pony that day?" Tristan asked.

He shook his head. "Nope," he said. "No grays."

Andi couldn't believe it. "Are you *sure*?" she said. "About fourteen hands, probably part Arabian?"

The kid shrugged. "Sure, I'm sure. Now, I've got to get back to work. Sorry I can't help."

"But it's *impossible*," Andi muttered as she and her friends shuffled out of the ring. "All the clues point to Perdita being one of Mrs. Osmond's ponies!"

"Sometimes clues aren't as good as they seem," Tristan said gloomily.

"How could we have been so wrong?" Natalie wondered aloud.

Andi shook her head. "I don't know, but we can't give up. We have to work harder to find even better clues," she said, determined. "We have to find Perdita's home or she'll have no place to go!"

Chapter Five

"Why didn't I take a picture of Perdita with my cell phone?" Natalie asked glumly as the kids waited for Mrs. O'Connor to pick them up. "Maybe the cowboy in the ring would have remembered her if we'd had something to show him."

"Let's take one when we get back to the riding center," Andi suggested. "We've still got time to make a few posters, right?"

Mrs. O'Connor's SUV crunched on the snow as it swung into the yard. "Any luck?" she called, leaning over to push open the car door.

"Nope." Neil climbed into the passenger seat and the others clambered into the back.

"It's awful," Andi burst out as Mrs. O'Connor pulled away. "Perdita's owner must be going crazy worrying about her. But none of our clues have turned up anything." She'd been so sure Mrs. Osmond was Perdita's owner, now she didn't know what to think. "Maybe we should look at a map of the area," she said at last. "It might give us a lead about where Perdita came from."

Mrs. O'Connor pulled into the riding center's driveway and everybody piled out and filed into the office.

Once inside, Neil pulled out a large map from his mother's desk drawer and laid it flat on the ground. They pored over it together, huddled close to the little heater that Mrs. O'Connor kept by her desk.

"She couldn't have come from that way," Andi pointed to the east, "unless she crossed the highway." It was horrible to think of Perdita dodging traffic on a busy road.

"There's a fence along that whole stretch of road," Neil said, shaking his head. "It's pretty unlikely."

"What about west?" Tristan suggested, studying that part of the map.

"See the ridges on the map?" Natalie pointed. "Those are mountains. And Perdita wasn't dirty or tired or anything—not like she climbed a mountain, anyway."

Andi traced a few fields north of the riding center. "How about here?"

Neil didn't seem convinced. "We know who owns those fields, and Mom's already called them."

There were no likely places to the south of the map, either. "Another dead end," Natalie sighed, sitting back on her heels.

"Let's go see how Perdita's doing," Andi suggested. "Maybe we'll get some fresh ideas when we see her."

Perdita hung her head over the stable door and whinnied when she saw them. Andi let herself into the stable with a body brush in her hand and started gently grooming the pony's mane.

"Aren't you afraid she'll bite you?" Tristan asked cautiously. He was watching from a safe distance on the other side of the door.

"No!" Andi laughed. "There's nothing to be worried about, Tris. Come and pet her. She'll love it."

Tristan edged toward the stable and reached out his hand to pet Perdita's nose. No sooner had he touched the pony than Perdita tossed her head and blew steam out of her nostrils. Tristan's hand flew back and he hit himself in the face. "Ow!"

Natalie burst out laughing. Andi and Neil joined in. It *was* pretty funny.

"You're scared of her, aren't you?" Natalie giggled.

"No. No way," Tristan said immediately, his eyes still watering. "She's just kind of . . . big. I don't want to get stepped on, okay?"

Andi traced the scar on the pony's withers with one finger. It reminded her of a jagged question mark. "How did you get that, then?" she murmured.

Perdita whickered softly in Andi's ear. "Perdita may not be able to talk," she said slowly as a plan began to form in her mind. "But she *can* still tell us stuff. How about we go back to the forest, like we did when we found the headcollar? Only this time, we take Perdita with us. Maybe she'll lead us back to where she came from."

"It's worth a shot," Neil agreed. "We could ride out there and—"

"Whoa," Tristan interrupted. "Ride? I'm not riding anything."

"Tristan *is* scared!" Natalie said in delight.

"I am *not*," Tristan said through gritted teeth. "I've just never done it before. There's a difference, you know?"

"We could put you on Donna—she's our gentlest pony and very used to beginners," Neil suggested. "How does that sound?"

Tristan looked extremely uneasy. "My dad's coming to get me at noon," he said. "We're going back to the Rain Forest Exhibition, to help Mr. Coombs with the snakes. I don't think I've got time to go riding, too."

"You are so weird, Tristan." Andi shook her head.

"You'll handle a dangerous snake, but you won't go near a pussycat like Donna?"

"She's a horse, not a cat," Tristan pointed out.

"Chicken!" Natalie burst out laughing. "*B-b-b-bock* . . . *bock, bock*! Here chickie, chickie . . ."

"Fine! I'll ride your horse," Tristan said, waving his arms in the air. "But I'm not doing any galloping."

"Cool. You know, the only time I've ridden a pony that's galloped off without any warning was when the pony saw a snake." Andi grinned. "Coincidence, huh?" She put her arm through Tristan's, to show him she was only teasing. "Come on," she said. "Let's go get set up."

"You're not thinking of riding Perdita, are you?" Mrs. O'Connor came across the yard as they were pulling down saddles, bridles, and girths from the tack room. "We don't know for sure if she's even been broken in."

"Don't worry, Mom," Neil said, slinging a saddle over his shoulder. "We're only going to lead her."

"Maybe I should stay here," Tristan began.

"Oh, no you don't!" Natalie poked him in the shoulder. "Pet Finders work together!"

Andi adjusted the saddle on Chipper's back. The feisty young gelding was becoming one of her favorite rides.

"Tristan, you'll find a helmet and some riding boots in

the equipment store next to the office," Neil said, tightening Flash's girth and returning to the tack room for Donna's saddle.

Tristan's eyes widened. "I need a *helmet*?"

Natalie checked out Tristan's head. "Don't worry about helmet hair," she advised. "Yours could use flattening, anyway."

When the horses were ready, Tristan gulped and mounted Donna.

As Neil led the gray mare out of the stable and down the narrow snow-packed path past the river, Andi and Natalie slowly rode their horses beside Tristan, encouraging him.

"Don't hold the reins so tight," Andi told him. "Loosen up a bit. Donna's not going to pitch you into the first ditch she sees."

"I'm not so sure," Tristan muttered. "She gave me a mean look when I got on."

"Probably doesn't like the way you smell," Natalie offered.

Andi laughed. It was clear that her best friend was enjoying a chance to get Tristan back for all his teasing about Neil.

They walked slowly along the frosty paddock in single

file. Neil and Perdita were leading the way and Tristan was safely sandwiched between Andi and Natalie. When they reached the trees, Andi watched Perdita intently to see how she reacted to being back in the forest.

"Make a right up ahead!" Neil called, turning Flash and Perdita to follow the track.

Andi turned Chipper's head by pulling gently on the right rein.

"*Right*, Tris!" she could hear Natalie calling at the back of the line. "Turn *right*, not left!"

"Try telling Donna that!" Tristan yelled. Looking over her shoulder, Andi saw Tristan sitting helplessly on Donna's back as the mare started veering off to the left.

"Pull on the right rein!" she shouted.

"Hey!" Tristan seemed surprised as Donna swung obediently to the right. He stared down at the reins with respect. "These things actually work!"

They walked on through the forest where the snow still lay thick on the ground, smooth and unmarked except for a few bird and animal tracks between the trees. At last, they reached the clearing where they had first seen Perdita.

Andi realized she was holding her breath as the mare warily snuffed the air. "Look, she's pulling that way!" she said excitedly, pointing toward a narrow track that disappeared through the pines.

Sure enough, Perdita was beginning to strain at her lead rope, flaring her nostrils and pricking her ears. Neil made a gentle clicking noise and let Perdita walk a bit ahead of Flash. Soon they were all following the track behind the mare, weaving along the snowy path. Andi wondered where they might end up. Could it be Perdita would be able to find her own way home after all?

They seemed to go on and on, trudging up unfamiliar slopes then slipping lightly down the other side, all while the gray mare snorted and pulled at her reins. Feeling cold and far from Hollow Creek, Andi was beginning to worry. Maybe they should head back before they got lost.

It was right then that she noticed a piece of fence off to the left, marking out a small patch of clear land among the trees. Snow was piled on the fencing struts like white icing on a cake.

"The fence is broken!" Natalie called over her shoulder, steering Tilly to a place where the rails had snapped. "See? Perdita could have gotten out here!"

"Nice catch," Neil said, and Natalie blushed to the roots of her hair.

Partway along the fence, two struts lay with their ends pointing down into the snow. It wasn't a large gap—was it big enough for a pony?

"Perdita definitely knows this place," Andi remarked. "Look at her!"

The mare's ears were still pricked. She looked confident and curious, as if she were familiar with her surroundings.

"There's a cabin," Tristan said suddenly.

Sure enough, a low-slung wooden cabin stood in the shadows beneath the trees on the far side of the clearing. Andi slid off Chipper's back and walked around the fence until she reached the cabin door. Lifting her hand, she knocked twice.

No answer.

Andi knocked again. There was no sound from inside the cabin. "Nothing," she said.

"Let's try the barn!" Tristan called, gingerly dismounting with Neil's help. "It's over there, to the right!"

The barn looked as run-down as the cabin. After securely tying the horses to a tree, Andi and the others walked up to the barn. Andi pushed open the door, which was hanging unevenly off its hinges. Inside there was some straw scattered on the floor. Bending down, Andi took a handful to study. It looked old and dusty.

"No sign of a horse here recently," Neil said, shaking his head.

"Trespassers!" shouted a voice behind them suddenly, making them leap out of their skin. "Trespassers, out!"

An old man with a bushy white beard stood glaring at them from the doorway. His beard and hair covered much of his face and he had a sharp eagle-beak of a nose.

"Who are you?" the man demanded. "What do you want?"

Andi stared at the man, frozen. "Sorry. We didn't think anyone was here—"

"What do you want?" the man repeated.

"We found a stray pony in the forest near your cabin. . . ." Natalie stuttered.

"Out!" the man repeated, advancing toward them.

"Better do what he says," Tristan muttered in a low voice. They began edging around the barn and back toward the door.

Andi tried again. "Have you lost a pony, sir? Only—"

"Can't stand horses," the man growled. "Can't stand people. Get out of here, I tell you! Out! Out! Out!"

"We're going!" Neil put his hands in the air. "Sorry!"

They fled the barn, hardly daring to look back over

their shoulders, as the man followed them out into the snow.

"And stay away from here!" the man shouted.

"Don't worry," Natalie muttered, untying Tilly with shaking fingers. "We're not coming anywhere near this place again."

Chapter Six

Once they were back on the path and headed toward the clearing, Andi began to feel her heartbeat returning to normal. The old man had looked half wild. She stared around at the endless, snowy expanse of trees. Maybe that was what happened when you lived out here, all alone. She shivered, imagining the dark, frozen nights and the endless stillness of the forest. Anyway, it was clear that the old barn hadn't been Perdita's home before they found her.

Gloomily, the group moved on in silence, along the track and across the paddock, until they were back at the riding center.

Perdita stood quietly, allowing Neil to take off her headcollar. She whickered at the other ponies who stood with their heads over their stable doors, then swung her head down to sniff at the quacking ducks that raced between her legs before disappearing into the barn.

Frustrated, Andi dismounted Chipper. "Who wouldn't claim such a beautiful pony?"

"Well, at least Perdita likes it here," Natalie remarked. "It's a shame she can't stay longer."

"You can say that again," Andi said. They watched as more ducks scurried past Perdita, who blew at them in a friendly manner over her stable door. "There must be something else we can think of." She carried Chipper's saddle and bridle back to the tack room. "What food does Perdita seem to like, Neil? Maybe we could track down the supplier or something." It was a long shot.

"She loves clover hay," said Neil, gesturing at the stuffed feed rack in Perdita's stable. "Just like most of the horses. No special brand. We just get it from the local supplier."

Andi's heart fell again. She felt like they were going around in hopeless circles.

"Hey," Tristan complained, still sitting high up on Donna's back. "Is anyone going to help me down?"

Neil gave Tristan a hand. Tris looked relieved to be back on solid ground again, but Andi noticed that he stroked Donna's neck as Neil led the gentle bay mare back to her stable.

"What time is it?" Tristan asked suddenly.

Andi checked her watch. "Almost twelve."

They all turned at the sound of tires crunching on the snow and gravel. Mr. Saunders swung into a parking space in a smoky cloud of exhaust.

"Right on cue!" Tristan rubbed his hands, looking enthusiastic as his dad switched off the engine. "We're heading back to the Rain Forest Exhibition this afternoon, remember? To help with the snakes!"

"Lucky you." Natalie rolled her eyes.

"Do you guys want a lift?" Tristan offered. "Dad'll drop you back home if you want."

Sitting in the back of Mr. Saunders' car ten minutes later, Andi watched the snowy landscape rushing away from her, leaving Hollow Creek in the distance beneath its backdrop of snowy mountains. She thought of the old man again, living alone in the forest.

"Why do you think that old guy in the woods lives that way?" she asked the others. "It must get real lonely out there."

"That guy was crazy," said Natalie with a shudder.

The car radio crackled into the news then. *"Reports are coming in about an incident at the Science Museum this morning, involving one of the reptiles. The museum is temporarily closing its exhibition. We'll keep you updated as the story develops."*

"An *incident*?" Andi sat up. "What's that all about?"

"Don't know," said Mr. Saunders with a frown. "But it looks like we aren't getting into the exhibition today."

"We have to!" Tristan cried. "Mr. Coombs is waiting for me!"

"Sounds like he'll have his hands full dealing with this incident—whatever it is," Natalie said.

"Please, Dad!" Tristan begged. "Let's just swing by. I've got to know what's going on."

Mr. Saunders shrugged. "We can try, but if they don't want visitors right now, we'll have to turn right around and head home."

"I don't mind," Tristan agreed. "I just want to know if the snakes are okay."

They drove on in silence. Andi's mind ran through the various possibilities. Maybe a tank had a leak—or maybe a rain-forest spider had bitten a visitor?

When they reached the Science Museum, there were tons of photographers, TV cameras, and journalists on the wide steps that led up to the double doors. They were all stamping their feet and looking cold. Police officers stood around talking into their radios. Anyone coming in or out of the museum was stopped and questioned by the press. Andi could tell something big was going on.

Then a man with a bullhorn began to shout. "Keep clear!" he barked from the museum's entrance. "Stay back! A boa constrictor has escaped from the exhibition. I repeat, keep clear!"

"That's Emerald! Let's check it out!" Tristan started to open the car door.

"Are you nuts?" Natalie's eyes were wide as she grabbed Tristan's sleeve. "Didn't you hear that announcement?"

"You heard the man," Mr. Saunders added. "And you know how dangerous boa constrictors are—"

"Only if you don't know what you're doing!" Tristan interrupted. "Dad, you know I understand snakes. Maybe we can do something to find Emerald!"

"Who's Emerald?" Mr. Saunders asked, sounding confused.

"The boa," Andi said, glancing at Tristan for confirmation. "We saw her on Saturday. She was the only one in the exhibition, right, Tris?"

Tristan nodded. "In this cold weather, a snake can freeze to death!"

"Mr. Coombs might appreciate some help," Andi said bravely. "The sooner they find Emerald, the better."

"I don't want to go anywhere near a snake," Natalie began. "Once is enough."

Tristan turned in his seat. "Pet Finders find pets to-gether! You said that to me about two hours ago, Nat. Horses, snakes—the same rules apply, right?"

"I guess," said Natalie in a small voice.

All three Pet Finders exited the car to see what they could do.

"Isn't that Simon?" Andi asked when they'd reached the steps. She pointed out the small boy with glasses they'd met at the exhibition the day before. He was searching the crowd as if he were looking for someone.

"Great," Tristan muttered. "The snake geek. I hoped he'd forget about today."

Andi was about to point out that Tristan was just as much of a snake geek, when Simon spotted them and hurried over.

"Hello," he said. "I've tried to find Mr. Coombs but I can't get through the press on the steps. Awful about Emerald, isn't it?"

A frightened-looking woman pushed past them, hud-dled deep in her coat. Everywhere Andi looked, she saw expressions of fear and bewilderment. The noise from the press grew louder.

"What have they done to find her so far?" Tristan asked, raising his voice to make himself heard.

"I don't know," Simon answered. "I've asked the

police, but they just looked at me like I was an annoying little kid."

Tristan pulled himself up to his full height. "I'll talk to them," he said kindly. "Maybe they'll listen to me."

"Look, there's Mr. Coombs!" Andi said. "Let's go ask *him* what's going on." She pointed out the man with the trimmed blond beard who had talked to them. He was trying to come down the steps, fighting his way through a group of reporters with microphones.

"Is the snake still inside the museum, or could it have escaped?"

"Is it a danger to the public, Mr. Coombs?"

"How could such a dangerous animal escape from the exhibition?"

"The boa constrictor is not dangerous," Andrew Coombs began, but the journalists interrupted him.

"There have been reports of a large snake attacking a dog in the neighborhood this morning . . ."

Spotting Andi and the others, Mr. Coombs pushed through the reporters and came down the steps. "It's nice to see some friendly faces," he said. "It's been crazy here all morning. The press want to turn this into some big scare."

"Do you have any clues?" Tristan asked. "Anything at all?"

Mr. Coombs scratched his head. "Nothing. We're guessing that the assistant who cleaned Emerald's enclosure last night didn't put the lid back on tight enough. When I came in today, she was missing. So, she must have escaped some time between six p.m. yesterday and eight this morning."

"We'd like to help look for her," Andi said firmly. "Where should we start?"

"That's very kind of you," Mr. Coombs began.

Andi sensed the word *but* coming next. "We've got lots of experience finding animals," she hurried on. "We told you yesterday about how we found those reptiles, remember? Tristan's got tons of experience with snakes, too." She glanced at the mob of reporters and cameras, adding, "It looks like you need all the help you can get."

"That's true," Mr. Coombs admitted. "Look, why don't you come in? We can talk more once we're out of this chaos."

Tristan nudged Andi happily as they all hurried up the steps behind Mr. Coombs. Simon straggled a little way behind.

"The power of the Pet Finders!" said Natalie.

Andi gave her an encouraging smile. It was clear that this was the last place on earth that Natalie wanted to be. "I'll go back and tell your dad we can stay a little longer, Tris," she said. "See you guys in there!"

Mr. Saunders was waiting by the curb, the motor idling and sending up puffs of exhaust into the cold air.

"Okay," he said when Andi had explained the situation. "I'll come pick you guys up in a couple of hours. Just don't get bitten, all right? Or else I'll have a whole lot of explaining to do to your moms."

Andi ran back up the steps as Mr. Saunders drove away. She found the others in the snake habitat section of the exhibit. Among a group of museum officials, all looking concerned and speaking together in low voices, Mr. Coombs was showing Tristan, Natalie, and Simon the lid of the enclosure. Sure enough, it was slightly ajar. Andi was surprised a snake the size of Emerald could fit through such a small gap.

"You're pretty close to the restrooms here, aren't you?" Tristan was asking, jotting something down in one of the red Pet Finders notebooks he always carried. Natalie was busy taking pictures of the scene with the tiny camera in her cell phone.

"They're just over there." Andrew Coombs pointed down the hall.

"Don't tell me," said Andi, with a nasty feeling in her stomach. "Emerald could have escaped through the restroom pipes?"

"It happens," Simon jumped in. "One time, I read

about an apartment block where a snake was living in the pipes. It kept popping out of the toilet bowls and freaking out the residents."

"I read that, too," Tristan said quickly.

Andi glanced at him. This competition thing with Simon was getting really boring.

Meanwhile, Natalie was looking faint.

"We did consider that," Andrew Coombs said, leading them along the hall, "but we decided it was more likely Emerald escaped through the storage room, here."

Andi peered inside the little room, where brushes and toilet paper and bottles of cleaning products stood lined up on shelves. A series of wide air vents ran up the side of the wall. "Through these, right?" she guessed.

"Right," said Coombs. "We've searched the building from top to bottom, and there's no sign of her. There are other vents around the museum, but since these are the closest to the snake exhibition, we figured . . ." He paused, and looked grim. "Well, you do the math."

Andi swallowed. It couldn't be clearer. Emerald had escaped from the building—and now she was loose on the streets!

Chapter Seven

Tristan and Simon both started talking at once.

"She's probably burrowed a hole in the snow—"

"No, I think she would have headed back indoors, somewhere warm—"

They both stopped and glared at each other.

"I was first," Tristan snapped.

"So, what? My idea's better," Simon began, talking over Tristan again.

"You guys, cut it out!" Andi cried. "This isn't a competition. Emerald needs our help. We have to work together on this, not fight with each other."

Both boys turned bright red.

"Sorry," Tristan muttered.

"Me, too," Simon agreed.

"Okay, Simon. You go first," said Mr. Coombs as they walked together down a long corridor toward the door at the back of the museum. He carried a special handling stick over his shoulder: a long, slender tool with a two-pronged curve at one end.

"I thought maybe Emerald would try and get inside again, once she figured how cold it was outdoors," Simon said, following Mr. Coombs as he pushed open a set of fire doors and stepped outside.

Mr. Coombs stood aside to let them out into the brisk, chilly wind. "The problem with that idea is the size of the museum grounds," he said, sweeping the air with his hand. "They're huge. Emerald would have gotten lost just trying to find somewhere warm."

"Could Emerald have gone straight back inside the museum?" Andi suggested.

"We thought of that," said Mr. Coombs. "But every inch of the building has been searched. It's looking unlikely."

Simon fell silent. Andi stared at the museum's sloping lawn, thick shrubbery, and winding paths, all blanketed in white.

"Let's look for tracks," Natalie suggested.

"Good idea," Andi agreed. "With snow like this, we'll have to be able to find a snake's winding print."

But Mr. Coombs shook his head. "The snow didn't stop falling until after eight this morning," he said. "We know

Emerald was gone by eight. Any tracks she made are long gone." He turned to Tristan. "What was your idea?"

"Well," said Tristan slowly, "I remember reading about how snakes burrowed underground to stay warm. They do it in Arizona in the winter—to stay torpid until it's warm enough to come out again."

"Torpid?" Natalie echoed, sounding puzzled.

"Keeping very still so they don't lose body heat by moving around," Andi explained. Her dad, who lived in Arizona, had told her about the habits of local reptiles.

"Burrowed under the snow." Andrew Coombs was nodding. "Smart thinking, Tristan. That's just the kind of behavior you might expect from a boa. Walk carefully now, guys. You don't want to step on her by mistake."

"No kidding," Natalie muttered, walking very close to Andi as they trudged up the sloping lawn looking for any unusual lumps or bumps beneath the snow.

"Mr. Coombs? Andrew Coombs!"

Andi's heart sank. One of the reporters from the front of the museum was making his way toward them. A cameraman and a sound operator were trailing behind him. "Mr. Coombs? James Henry, Fast Track News. May we have a word? Have you found the killer snake yet?"

"Watch where you're walking!" Mr. Coombs said, holding up his hand.

The reporter stopped abruptly and stared in horror at his feet. Hampered by their equipment, the cameraman and the sound operator crashed into him and nearly sent him flying. Andi found it hard not to laugh.

The reporter looked up, flustered. "Would you care to make a statement?" he asked. "Something reassuring for our viewers? For example, if a member of the public is bitten, would an antidote be made available to them?"

"Boa constrictors aren't poisonous," Simon said hotly.

"Thanks, kid." James Henry waved his hand, as if this information was unimportant. "Have the emergency rooms in area hospitals been made aware of the situation?"

"Please!" Mr. Coombs began.

"Andi, Nat!" Tristan gave a shout. "Over here!"

Andi rushed to where Tristan was kneeling in the snow, the others close behind her. Several inches below the heavy white surface, something brown could be glimpsed.

"Start rolling, Clyde!" James Henry instructed the cameraman. He cleared his throat and nodded at the sound operator.

Andi's heart was in her mouth as Mr. Coombs gently pushed the snow away with the hook on the end of the handling stick—then reached down, twisting the stick very slightly to get a better grip on the reptile.

"As you can see behind me," James Henry said into the camera, "a delicate operation is underway. Anthony Coombs—"

"*Andrew* Coombs," Andi corrected, looking up.

James Henry looked irritated as the cameraman lowered the lens. "From the top again," he ordered, straightening his tie.

"No need," came Andrew Coombs's voice. Andi and the reporter looked around. Dangling from the handler's stick was a fat, dead piece of wood.

"Terrific," James Henry grumbled as Tristan went scarlet with embarrassment. "Now what do I tell my editor?"

"Tell him the truth," Andi suggested. "The snake is still on the loose, but it isn't dangerous."

"Sure, kid." The reporter slid his pen in his top pocket. "Don't forget to tune in to Fast Track this afternoon. At four o'clock, greater Seattle will know exactly what we're dealing with."

Later that day, Andi, Natalie, and Tristan were all sitting in Andi's bedroom on Aspen Drive. Andi was hunched over her computer, with Buddy curled up cozily on her feet.

"There," she said with satisfaction, hitting the PRINT button. The printer began to spit out Pet Finders posters of Perdita, using the cell phone picture Natalie had taken earlier. "We can put these around the neighborhood tomorrow."

Tristan checked his watch. "It's almost four o'clock. Let's go catch the news."

Down in the living room, the Fast Track logo was already splashed across the screen. James Henry's face appeared, grave and formal. *"This afternoon, Orchard Park faces one of its most dangerous civil situations ever,"* he said soberly. *"A boa constrictor, hungry and perhaps liable to attack, escaped from the Science Museum this morning and is now roaming the streets, unchecked and unfettered."*

Andi stared at the screen in disbelief. He made Emerald sound terrifying!

"That's not true!" Tristan shouted at the screen. "Boas don't attack anyone unless they're provoked!"

"Police are asking for calm," James Henry's voice continued as the camera panned across Orchard Park's deserted streets. *"If you see or hear any clues as to where this twelve-foot beast may be, here's where to call."* A telephone number flashed onto the screen. *"This is James Henry, reporting for Fast Track News."*

Andi flipped off the TV in disgust. "I knew we couldn't trust him!"

"It's too late," Natalie said in a low voice. "The damage is done."

Tristan was pacing the living room. "This is awful!" he said. "Now everybody is going to think Emerald is out to get them. The boa is in more danger than ever! We have to go back to the museum and help look for her again tomorrow."

"We have to be at Hollow Creek in the morning," said Natalie anxiously. "It's already Tuesday, and we still haven't cracked Perdita's case."

"The stabling problem's not going to go away," Andi added. "And remember—the museum staff and the Orchard Park police are out looking for Emerald. We're Perdita's only hope."

Tristan battled with his feelings. "Fine," he said at last. "I'll go to the museum, you two go to Hollow Creek. But we have to meet up after lunch, okay? We need everyone on this, guys. And I mean *everyone*."

On Tuesday morning, the bitter wind had died down and the sun was shining weakly in the February sky as Mrs. Peters dropped Andi and Natalie off at Hollow Creek.

"Tell me again," Andi prompted Natalie as they hurried across the yard toward the riding center office. "You called two more auction houses about Perdita yesterday afternoon?"

"Uh-huh." Natalie nodded. "My stepdad keeps the phone books for all of Washington State in his office. So I did some detective work on my own, finding other auction houses that aren't listed in the Seattle area phone book. One of the auction houses said they'd call me back this morning with any news." She patted her cell phone, which was tucked in her coat pocket.

Neil stepped out of the office as Andi and Natalie reached the steps. "No Tristan today?" he asked, glancing behind them.

"He went back to the Science Museum to help look for the missing snake," Andi explained. "If anyone can find Emerald, Tristan can." She spoke with more conviction than she felt. The museum grounds were enormous, and another night had passed with no sign of Emerald.

She held out a Perdita poster to Neil. "We already put up a dozen of these in town this morning. Maybe you could put one on the bulletin board in the office? Then we can start making a few more calls about Perdita."

Neil took the poster then gestured to a set of forks and spades leaning against the side of the stable block. "We need to muck out the stables first," he said apologetically. "Keeping the horses inside during this kind of weather makes a whole lot more work. They're out in the paddock this morning, so can you give me a hand? I'll just go put this poster up in the office."

With a sigh, Andi took up a spade. Natalie was about to do same when her cell phone rang. With an undisguised look of relief on her face, Natalie answered the call.

"The Pet Finders Club, Natalie speaking. Yes?"

Andi began shoveling out the first stable, keeping her ears firmly trained on Natalie and her phone conversation. It took her mind off the smell.

"Guess what?" Natalie's eyes were lit with excitement as she snapped her phone shut. "That was the auction house I was telling you about. A nearby breeding center lost five horses the other day when some prankster opened the corral. Green Fields Stud Farm—I wonder if Neil's heard of it? I'll go find him."

She hurried away, her blond ponytail swinging down the back of her white padded jacket. Wondering how Natalie managed to stay so clean in the mucky stable yard, Andi dug one more shovel full of soiled straw, then leaned her spade against the wall and followed her friend.

Neil was in Perdita's stable, shoveling straw.

"Sure, I know Green Fields," he said, straightening up. "Kind of pricey, but they have great stock. I'm surprised my mom didn't think to call them herself." He reeled off the number, and Natalie made a call.

"No answer," Natalie said after a couple of minutes.

"Probably mucking out the stalls, just like we are," Andi replied.

"Maybe we could pay a visit," Neil suggested. "It's not too far—there's a bus that stops at the end of our driveway that would take us straight there."

"That's fine by me," said Natalie, pocketing her phone.

Andi nodded. "Me, too."

"I'll go check out the timetable in Mom's office."

As Neil strode away, Natalie leaned in close to Andi. "Perfect," she said with a smile. "It gets us out of this dirty work!"

Green Fields was farther out of town than Hollow Creek. Andi watched the mountains growing closer as the bus flew down the highway, the trees growing higher and thicker with every mile.

"This is my kind of place," Natalie said as they got off the bus and stood beneath a large wrought-iron gate. She was admiring the sweep of graveled yard, the neatly painted stables, and the sturdy new fencing that marked out the level paddocks. "Not that Hollow Creek isn't great, too," she added quickly, glancing at Neil.

As far as Andi could tell, Natalie's crush was showing no signs of going away any time soon. They walked up the driveway, feeling the crunch of compacted snow and gravel beneath their feet. Andi felt a little intimidated by the grandness of Green Fields, and she was horribly aware of her filthy jeans.

"Yes?" a woman called as she strode toward them. She was tall and thin, with high cheekbones and graying hair tucked into a dark green headscarf. "Are you looking for someone?" She stopped in front of them, her hands on her hips.

"Well," Andi began, "we kind of wondered if *you* were. A pony, I mean." That had come out wrong, she realized.

"We've found an Arabian pony," said Neil. "Gray, fourteen hands high? We heard you had a break out recently."

The woman gave a brisk bark of laughter. "You make Green Fields sound like some kind of prison. Yes, we lost a number of animals for a short time, but we only have horses here."

Perdita is *a horse*, Andi thought, puzzled. But somehow she knew it would be the wrong thing to say to this woman.

Sensing Andi's confusion, Neil stepped in. "Nothing under fourteen point two hands, right?" he said. Andi remembered that a horse below that height was officially called a pony. She was glad that she hadn't said anything.

"Right." The woman gazed at them, her hands still on her hips. "And no grays among them. Was there anything else?"

Andi found her voice. "Did you find all your missing horses?"

"Every one," the woman nodded. "They hadn't gone far, and the boundary fence is secure so there was no possibility of them getting onto the road. Sorry you wasted your time." With that, she turned and walked back to the stables as purposefully as she had approached them in the first place.

Back at Orchard Park after lunch, Andi and Natalie walked their dogs through the park. As Buddy and Jet frolicked in the snow, kicking up sprays of white flakes with their paws, Andi felt gloomy. They had found a bunch of clues in connection with Perdita, but not one of them had told them anything. Time was ticking away for the gray mare, and the case hadn't even gotten off the ground!

"I guess we could go back to Green Fields and ask if they know of anywhere that breeds ponies with Arabian blood," Natalie suggested.

Andi shuddered at the thought of talking to that woman again. There had been something very intimidating about how efficiently she had dismissed them. "I'd rather be eaten by Emerald." She stopped and sighed, wondering how Tristan was doing at the museum.

As if in answer to her thoughts, Tristan came panting up the hill toward them. To Andi's surprise, Simon was right behind him.

"Thank goodness you're here!" Tristan stopped, panting and putting his hand on his side. "You remember Simon, right? We met up at the museum again today. I figured we needed all the help we could get, so I invited him over. I've been calling and calling, Nat, but there was no answer."

Natalie pulled out her cell phone. "Oh," she said, "dead battery. I guess I used it a little too much today."

Tristan waved a hand. "It doesn't matter. Have you seen today's paper?"

Andi and Natalie shook their heads.

"We went straight over to Hollow Creek after breakfast," Andi said. "It's bad, right?"

Simon thrust the newspaper under Andi's nose. "We picked up this on our way out of the museum this morning. Read it!"

"*Serpent Terror On Peaceful Streets*," Andi read with a sinking heart. It had been bad hearing it on the news last night. It was even worse seeing it in print.

"Go on," said Tristan, sounding furious.

" '*Police are baffled as to the whereabouts of a dangerous boa constrictor, which escaped from the poorly secured Rain Forest Exhibition at the Science Museum yesterday morning,*' " Andi read. " '*The beast is over twelve feet long, and likely to attack since its last meal was several days ago.*' But that's not true!"

"She's only eight feet three inches," Simon said, nodding. "And she won't get hungry until at least Friday. Boas are really gentle — they're afraid of human contact, actually, and avoid it if they can."

"This is awful!" Andi cried. "What if someone reads this and then sees Emerald?"

Tristan nodded. "They'll panic," he said. "And worse than that, they may even try to kill her!"

Chapter Eight

Back in the warmth of Andi's home on Aspen Drive, the Pet Finders and Simon headed to Andi's room. They surfed the Internet in search of more news about Emerald, trying to make sense of the headlines. There were stories of snake sightings—in someone's hot tub in their yard, in a tiny garden shed, and even on someone's front porch. Andi sighed, imagining the reporters sharpening their pencils for more scare stories tomorrow.

Natalie shuddered. *"'Squeezed to Death!'"* she read. "Apparently they think Emerald killed a dog not far from the museum. How horrible!"

"You're not falling for that, are you, Nat?" Tristan asked. "It's clear none of these reporters know the first thing about snakes. It's careless reporting, if you ask me."

"And it's the worst thing that could have happened

for Emerald," Andi said. She glanced out of the window. It was getting dark and snow was falling again, thicker than ever. "If the boa sneaks inside somewhere to get warm, she'll be in just as much danger as if she were out in the snow."

"Guys, I think I've got something." Natalie looked up from the computer. "Maybe there's some kind of pattern," she suggested. "Look—all these articles mention streets where Emerald has been sighted. Maybe we can figure out where to start looking for her?"

Andi stared at her best friend. "That's an idea."

Natalie seemed pleased, and casually flicked her ponytail over her shoulder.

"So, who's got a detailed map of Orchard Park?" Andi asked, looking around the room. "One with more than highways and mountains."

Tristan's eyes lit up. "My parents have all kinds of maps back home!" he exclaimed. "One of them lists all the street names and everything. Let's head over there and see if we can make some kind of pattern out of the sightings. Have you got Mr. Coombs's number, Simon? Let's call and check on those addresses and see if he knows exactly which houses they're talking about."

Andi scribbled down the list of addresses as Natalie read them from the Internet articles. Simon then phoned

Mr. Coombs, who gave them clearer information about the addresses where sightings had been reported: 1050 Duke Avenue, 1105 Prince Street, 1238 Earl Drive, 1347 Queen's Lane.

"It's like some kind of royalty roll call," Tristan joked as they stared at the finished list. "I'm pretty sure these are all at the far end of town, not far from the museum. Mom and Dad's map will tell us more." He glanced at Simon. "Are you coming, too?"

"I've got to go home," Simon said regretfully. "But thanks for letting me help out," he added. "It's been really cool." He cleared his throat. "Oh, and Tristan?"

"Yeah?"

"You know that story I told in the museum the other day? The one about a boa eating a man?" he asked. Tristan nodded. "Well, I kind of—made it up. To look good, I guess. Sorry about that."

"Did you make up the one about the snake in the sewer, too?" Natalie asked hopefully.

Simon looked more cheerful. "Nope. That one totally happened."

"Don't worry about it," Tristan said gruffly. "We all do silly things sometimes."

Then Andi remembered that Tristan had claimed to know the same fact about the man-eating snake. She tried hard not to grin. "Poor kid," she said, as they waved good-bye to Simon five minutes later. "I don't think he has many friends."

"What do you expect from a snake geek?" said Tristan, reaching for his coat hanging in the porch.

"You're the one who invited him over," Natalie reminded him. She pulled on a white hat with furry pom-poms dangling from the top.

Tristan grinned. "Snake geeks stick together, that's what I always say."

They trudged through the pelting snow to the Saunders' house. True to Tristan's word, there was an enormous map of Orchard Park hanging in the study. It was framed in heavy wood and glass.

"No one's home," Tristan announced. "My parents must still be at work, and I guess my brother's got a date." Pulling open the desk drawer, he took out a red marker pen and uncapped it. He marked the first snake-sighting address on the glass over the map, putting a bright red X on Duke Avenue.

"Are you sure we should write on that map?" Andi asked cautiously, taking off her coat. Buddy yapped and started licking at his snow-covered feet.

"My dad does it all the time when he's checking out the real estate market. It wipes off." Tristan studied the

list of snake-sighting addresses, his pen poised over the map. "1238 Earl Drive," he said. "That's about halfway down the block." He made a brisk circle around the address, then another at 1347 Queen's Lane.

"Is that the museum?" Natalie tapped at a building circled by a wide green block of garden on the far right of the map.

Tristan nodded.

Andi noticed that Earl Drive and the rest of them stood behind the museum, tucked right up in the northwest-hand corner of the town. She thought about Emerald escaping through the air vents in the little storage room. The storage room had lain at the back of the museum, hadn't it?

"What do you think you're doing, Tristan?"

Andi turned around to see Mr. Saunders standing in the door of the study.

"Oh, hi, Dad," said Tristan. "We're marking out places where Emerald has been seen. What's the matter?"

Mr. Saunders strode over and removed the pen from Tristan's hand. "With my permanent marker?" he said, studying the pen in horror.

"No, it's not permanent. It'll rub off," Tristan said. He ran his finger over the largest red circle. "See? Um..."

"Oh, yes," Mr. Saunders said as they all stared at the

still perfect red circle on the glass. "I see plenty. I see the rest of your evening in here with glass cleaner."

"But . . . but . . ." Tristan said weakly, rubbing at the pen marks with the sleeve of his sweater and getting nowhere. "Maybe I used the wrong pen."

"We're really sorry, Mr. Saunders," said Andi, feeling very embarrassed. "We thought—"

"Don't worry, Andi," Mr. Saunders sighed, running his hand through his gray hair. He raised his eyebrows at Tristan, who trudged out of the study in search of the glass cleaner.

"I'll put some food on," Mr. Saunders said, shaking his head in a resigned way. "You two staying for dinner?"

"Thanks, but I think we'd better head home," Andi said. "The snow is getting pretty bad out there."

Lifting his head from where he had been licking at a clump of snow stuck to his belly, Buddy barked in agreement.

"I'll give you all a ride," Mr. Saunders offered. "When the weather does this, it's easy to get lost, even in familiar places."

Tristan had found the glass cleaner and was standing in the door of the study, scowling at the map.

"Tris?" Natalie asked, pulling her coat back on. "While you're cleaning that off, could you figure out a search route? We can meet up first thing tomorrow morning and look for Emerald."

"But . . ." Andi bit back her anxiety about Perdita. Tomorrow was Wednesday, which left them only three more days to find Perdita's owner. *We don't have any leads*, she reminded herself. *We have to wait for a call from Neil.*

"Sure," Tristan said grumpily. "Call me in the morning, okay? Assuming I can clean this stuff off tonight, of course. I might be here till the end of winter break."

The next morning, the snow was so deep that Andi had to help her mom shovel it out of the driveway to get the car out of the garage. Buddy thought it was a great game and barked at the tip of Andi's shovel every time it came out of the snowdrifts.

"Phew," Judy Talbot sighed, straightening up and rubbing at the small of her back. "At times like these, I wish we were back in Florida."

"It's better than shoveling muck at Hollow Creek," Andi confided in her mom as she headed into the garage to put the shovels away. "Mom, are you sure you have time to drop me off at the museum today?"

"My first meeting isn't until ten," Mrs. Talbot replied, opening the passenger door. "Besides," she added with a smile, "Orchard Park looks pretty in all this snow."

"So much for wanting to be back in Florida!" Andi laughed, sliding across the backseat and pulling her scarf tightly around her neck. Buddy bounded in after her with one leap.

Andi's cell phone rang. It was Natalie.

"Bad news," Natalie said breathlessly. "I just got a call from Neil."

Andi sat up. "Did something happen to Perdita?" she asked in horror.

"No, she's fine," Natalie assured. "It's Mr. Forster. He moved his booking up. He wants the O'Connors to start stabling his horse on *Friday* instead of Monday!"

Andi gasped. That meant three days less to find Perdita's owner—and they still had no leads. It was the worst possible news. "He can't do that!" she protested, gripping the phone.

Natalie sounded close to tears. "What are we going to do, Andi?"

Andi made a decision. "Call Tristan. Tell him that we have to go to Hollow Creek right now," she said.

"But Emerald—" Natalie began.

"Emerald has all of Orchard Park looking for her," Andi reminded her firmly. "Perdita only has us."

"Okay," Natalie said. "I'll call him, then call you back."

"Change of plans, Mom." Andi shoved the phone back in her pocket. "Can you take me to Hollow Creek instead?"

"Yes, ma'am." Mrs. Talbot saluted and turned the car around.

Andi's cell rang again. "It's all good," Natalie told her. "Christine Wilson called Tristan just before I spoke to him. She needs his help at Paws for Thought today, so he wasn't going to be able to look for Emerald, anyway. He says good luck, and he'll see us later."

The snow started falling again as Mrs. Talbot drove along the familiar road to the riding center. Curled up on the warm backseat of the car, Andi found herself thinking of the strange old man they'd seen the other day, all alone in his cabin in the middle of the forest. It had snowed so hard in the night and showed no sign of letting up. Perhaps he'd been snowed in? She shivered at the thought of being alone up there, cut off from everything.

Andi found Neil grooming Perdita in the stables. "I heard about Mr. Forster," she told him.

Perdita nuzzled into Neil's shoulder. "Usually getting a horse in for livery is great news and getting them early is even better," he said. "But right now . . ." He stared somewhere over Perdita's head, deep in thought. The mare blew softly through her nostrils and butted at the pocket of his jacket. Neil pulled out a carrot, which Perdita munched contentedly.

Andi swallowed. Poor Neil. It was clear he was getting really attached to Perdita. "At least she's warm and safe for now," she pointed out. "Imagine if we'd never found her? She'd have frozen to death for sure." She stared at the forest and thought about the old man again. His clothes had been thin and frayed, and his broken-down old cabin had looked far colder than Perdita's cozy stable.

"Earth to Andi." Neil snapped his fingers in her face. "You were miles away just now. What were you thinking about?"

"That old guy in the woods," Andi admitted. "It must be awful to be stuck out there on your own in this weather. Do you think he's okay?"

"He was mean and crazy, remember?" Neil protested. "Are you saying you want to go check on him?"

"Sort of." Andi knew she sounded nuts. But she couldn't get the old man out of her head.

The snow had stopped for the moment. There was

a crunch of tires on the gravel, and Mrs. Peters swung up the driveway in her pale gold Jeep. Natalie hopped out, pulling her cream-colored jacket tightly around her. "Any news?" she asked hopefully, running over to Andi and Neil.

"How's this for news?" Neil said. "Andi wants to go check on that crazy old guy who chased us out of his barn the other day."

Natalie's eyes nearly popped out of her head. "Are you *serious*? We're supposed to be worried about Perdita, not that creepy man!"

"Come on!" Andi tried to explain. "He's on his own. He might be out of food or freezing to death in that old cabin. Anyway, we never got to ask him about Perdita, did we? If we take some food for him, maybe he'll be a little more—welcoming. He might give us the lead we need."

"Good point," Neil said after a moment. "We can't take the horses, though, and walking will be very hard—the snow is too deep. I'll ask Mom if we can dig out the cross-country skis that she keeps in the barn. They'll get us there."

In the barn, the goats bleated and shuffled around as Mrs. O'Connor gave Neil two old blankets, some cans of soup, and a few loaves of bread for the man. Meanwhile, Andi and Natalie wrestled with the complicated bindings on their skis.

"These things are huge!" Andi groaned. "They must be a couple of yards long, at least."

"Best thing for cross-country." Neil grinned. "Here, let me show you how to strap them on."

Andi struggled to keep her balance on the skis as Neil looped the bindings around her feet. Testing them, she found that she could move the back of her foot off the ski, but not the front. She tried sliding across the barn floor—without much success.

"Catch!" Neil tossed Andi and Natalie some of the soup and bread to shove in their backpacks. Then he handed them each a pair of ski poles, so they could push themselves across the snow. "Okay? Let's go."

Once they were on the snow, Andi found the skis easier to manage. They glided over the deep drifts, making a soothing *shush* noise. Andi discovered that she could move faster by lifting the back of her foot off the ski each time she took a step.

The forest was even more hushed than it had been on Monday, the tree branches more heavily bowed with snow than before. Natalie stayed clear of the heaviest looking ones as they skied along in silence. When they reached the clearing where they'd found Perdita, the little track leading over the slopes and to the cabin was almost completely invisible beneath the snow.

"Looks like he still hasn't fixed his fence," Neil observed as they reached the little cabin with its barn and paddock. "We never did find out if Perdita broke that, did we?"

The three of them skied up to the cabin, then looked nervously at one another. Andi found the courage to knock. The door opened almost immediately, groaning against the weight of snow piled up outside.

"The trespassers return," the old man growled. "What is it this time?"

Well, at least he wasn't holding his gun and he hadn't tried to chase them away. With fumbling fingers, Andi pulled off her backpack and took out some soup and bread. "We wondered if you might need these," she said, holding them out to the man. "Seeing how you're snowed in, and . . ." She trailed off, unsure of the man's expression. "We have blankets, too," she added lamely.

"Well," the man said at last, "that's mighty kind of you. I was running low on supplies. Care to come in?"

Inside, the cabin was spotless and cozy. Andi blinked in surprise, taking in the carved wooden furniture, the little radio perched on a windowsill, the neatly stacked logs by the blazing fireplace, and, most surprising of all, a state-of-the-art laptop set up on a wooden table beside a window overlooking the paddock.

"Take a seat," said the old man, waving at a couple of chairs beside the fireplace. "Warm yourselves up a bit. My name's Race. Race Clarkwell."

Andi and the others introduced themselves as well. "Race?" Andi asked. It was an unusual name.

"Horatio to my mother," said the man. "Race to everybody else."

"We're glad you're okay, Mr. Clarkwell," said Natalie. "Sorry about the misunderstanding last time."

Race Clarkwell waved his hand. "Don't apologize," he said, a little gruffly. "I don't get many visitors, see. Can I get you a drink?"

He was a nature journalist, he told them over steaming mugs of hot cocoa. "Came out here twenty years ago, never looked back. Magazines always want articles on woodlands and animals and such. You see plenty in a place like this."

"Don't you get lonely?" Andi couldn't help asking.

Race Clarkwell looked surprised. "Why would I be lonely? I have the trees and the deer. Sometimes there are bears. It's a pretty crowded neighborhood."

"Do you have a horse?" Neil asked. "We saw your paddock and wondered."

"A long time ago," said Race Clarkwell abruptly. "I think the horse got more lonely than I ever did. She died seven years back."

Andi put down her mug. Mr. Clarkwell had obviously cared deeply for his horse. It looked like it was still painful for him to talk about it. "Did you see a pony near your cabin, about three or four days ago?" she asked as gently as she could.

Mr. Clarkwell frowned. "There *was* a little pony," he said. "Color of snow. Seemed pretty spooked by something. Friday afternoon, I think it was."

Friday—the day of the trailer accident! Andi leaned forward eagerly. "That's her! Was she—did you notice anyone with her?"

The old man shook his head. "Not a soul but her," he said. "Couldn't get near. She was puffing and blowing and skipping around like a ballerina. Headcollar was trailing some kind of rope. She was twitching her head like she was trying to shake the darn thing off. What's this about, anyway?"

Andi explained the situation, her mind racing back to the auction yard. But then there was Eddie, the guy from the truck who had sworn there'd been no grays in the trailer that day of the accident. Could he have been lying about it? But why?

"Do you remember the exact time you saw the pony, Mr. Clarkwell?" Natalie asked. "If you saw her after the trailer accident, it's another clue that she may have come from the auction yard."

Race Clarkwell leaned over to his laptop and clicked a couple of buttons. "I was finishing a piece about the woodland caribou at the time," he said thoughtfully. A picture of a fine-looking stag with curved antlers and a thick white ruff of fur around his neck appeared on the screen. He scrolled down a list of files. "Looks like I saved that piece at three thirty-four p.m. on Friday afternoon," he said. "Any good?"

"We'll check out the exact time of the accident," Andi promised, her mind whirling. Hopefully this was the clue they needed to solve the mystery of Perdita once and for all.

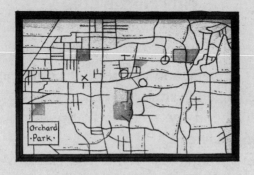

Chapter Nine

"We still can't be sure," Tristan argued, lying full length on the fireside rug at Andi's house that evening. He'd finished work at Paws for Thought right after Andi and Natalie got back to Aspen Drive and had come over as fast as he could. "You said that guy at the auction yard insisted he hadn't seen a gray that day. And why would he lie about it? Maybe Perdita got lost around the same time as the accident, and the crash just scared her deeper into the forest."

Andi's head was spinning. "But the rest of the evidence seems so clear!" she exclaimed. "You saw that other article about the trailer accident that we pulled off the Internet just now. It said that the accident happened at *three-fifteen*. Nineteen minutes later Perdita is jumping around in Mr. Clarkwell's backyard. It all fits!

We have to go back and talk to that Eddie guy again. If only he'll change his story."

"You can't bend the facts to fit the search," Tristan said, shaking his head.

Andi knew Tristan was right. You can't twist the details just because you want a different outcome. The problem was that the clues had run dry, and now Andi, Tristan, and Natalie had no clue what to do next.

Andi rolled irritably onto her back. Buddy promptly put his paws on her chest and started licking her face. It was hard to stay angry with a cute little dog tickling her chin. "Since you mention facts," Andi said, sitting up again and pushing Buddy away, "let's talk about Emerald. Any news today?"

"Everybody in Orchard Park's gotten so jittery about Emerald that people are calling the police about old branches lying around in their yards," Tristan said gloomily.

"Easy mistake to make," Andi grinned, poking Tristan in the ribs as she remembered his supposed sighting in the museum grounds.

Tristan ignored her. He pulled a new-looking map out of his pocket and spread it out on the rug. "According to the latest news, we have three more sightings," he said.

"They gave the house numbers this time. 1350 Queen's Lane, 1551 Monarch Way, and 1246 Earl Drive."

"Nice map," said Andi. "Where did you get it?"

Tristan gave a sheepish smile. "My folks bought it for me after the, uh, graffiti incident."

"Two of the streets are the same as last time," Andi pointed out. "The house numbers are close, too. That should double the chances of finding Emerald around there, don't you think?"

"Can I borrow your phone, Andi?" Tristan asked. "I want to call Simon and tell him the latest."

"At last, the snake geeks are buddies," said Natalie with a grin as Tristan talked to Simon on Andi's cell. "It's a match made in heaven. They can talk about venom and fangs all day long."

"Simon said he'd seen the articles already," said Tristan, hanging up and plunking himself back down on the rug. "And guess what? He already called Mr. Coombs at the museum to tell him about the new sightings being in the same places as before!"

"Why didn't he call us?" Natalie asked, looking annoyed. "We're the Pet Finders around here, not him."

"He tried to call me this afternoon, but there was no answer at home because I was at Paws for Thought,"

Tristan explained. "Anyway, Mr. Coombs had already figured it out himself, and they're laying on a search of the
area in the morning. Simon said Mr. Coombs wants us
all to go over and help!"

As Andi took out her coat and gloves on Thursday
morning, Buddy watched her mournfully from his bed.
Andi had decided to leave him home again. She'd given
him an extra tasty breakfast and a long walk, but it was
tough ignoring his hopeful eyes.

"I know it's winter break, Bud, and I should be spend-
ing more time with you," she said, hunkering down to
her dog's bed so she could scratch him between the
shoulders, in just the spot he liked. "But these animals
need me, okay?"

Buddy sighed and flopped down on his cushion. Pulling on her gloves and coat, Andi's thoughts kept drifting
back to Perdita. Even with Emerald to worry about today, it was impossible not to think about how the mare
could be homeless if they didn't find her owner within
the next twenty-four hours.

After Natalie and Tristan had left last night, Andi had
called every animal shelter in the Orchard Park area,
but none were set up to offer Perdita a stable. Costs at
the ranches near Hollow Creek were out of the ques-

tion. In desperation, Andi had started wondering if she could ask her mom to fix up the garage as a temporary shelter for the pony even though she knew that the answer would most certainly be no. It made Andi want to race back to Hollow Creek and retrace her steps a million times over. But without a new clue or a plan the Pet Finders would just be running in circles—and that was no help to anybody.

She shook her head and tried to focus on Emerald. The least she could do was help find the snake. Right now, the only new clues they had in their current cases were about the lost boa, so that's where they were headed—to the museum to help Mr. Coombs with the search.

"Rather you than me," said Mrs. Talbot, kissing Andi good-bye. "I'm glad Mr. Coombs is coming with you to handle that snake if you find her."

"Me, too," Andi agreed, with a shiver. "There's no way we could have handled an eight-foot boa on our own—even with Tristan and Simon knowing so much about snakes."

They both heard the honk of a horn. It was the Saunders's car, and Andi ran outside.

"Hurry up." Tristan opened the car door so Andi could slide inside. "Mr. Coombs arranged for the search to start at nine."

"Simon's meeting us there," Natalie added as Mr. Saunders pulled out of Aspen Drive and took the familiar road to the Science Museum.

Sure enough, Simon was waiting at the bottom of the museum steps, polishing his glasses. A handful of reporters were also standing on the steps, hoping for further news as they hugged cups of steaming coffee.

The kids ran around the back of the museum to meet Mr. Coombs. "Maybe when people see you kids helping with the search, they'll understand that there's nothing to be afraid of," he explained.

Andi noticed James Henry standing close by with his camera crew. She sighed.

"Hey, there," the reporter called in a hearty voice. "What are you doing here?"

"Helping with the search," Tristan said shortly.

James Henry raised his eyebrows. "Pretty scary for kids," he said. "Twelve feet of snake, ready to eat you from the toes up, huh?"

Andi looked at Tristan and Natalie and rolled her eyes.

"Emerald's eight feet three inches," Simon informed him. "And you're the most irresponsible reporter I've ever met!"

"No way. That thing is twelve feet and I can prove it!"

James Henry flipped wildly through his reporter's note-book then stopped suddenly on a page. He looked up and smiled weakly at the kids. "Oops. My mistake," he said with a chuckle. "Well, I guess it made for a more in-teresting story. You've got to keep your audience on the edge of their seats, you know."

"What a loser," Natalie whispered as they started walking toward Earl Drive with Mr. Coombs.

"Look on the bright side," Tristan said with a devilish grin. "Emerald might eat him."

They giggled, feeling a little better.

"This could work to our advantage," Andi pointed out. "If we find Emerald and show Mr. Henry that she's just a frightened animal who wouldn't hurt a fly, he'll have to admit his mistake on the air, won't he?"

"Don't count on it," Simon replied.

It was a ten-minute walk to the first address on the list—1350 Queen's Lane. The Pet Finders waited pa-tiently on the sidewalk as Mr. Coombs rang the bell, looking around at the big elegant houses with wrap-around porches that lined the street.

"No answer." Coombs rejoined them on the sidewalk. "The next one is just two blocks away."

Andi could hear James Henry talking in front of the

camera as he hurried behind them. "The thinly-staffed search operation from the Science Museum met its first obstacle when there was nobody home at the first witness address on their list. Could they be the snake's first human victims? Four schoolkids have joined the operation today, out for the thrill of the hunt. . . ."

They had no luck on Monarch Way, either.

"That reporter guy is really making my skin crawl," Tristan muttered to Andi as they walked to the end of Earl Drive to make their third call of the morning.

Looking up at the next address, Andi decided that 1246 Earl Drive was even cooler than the rest of the houses on the block. It was redbrick and looked quite old, with neatly painted white woodwork and a huge porch with fluted columns.

The door was opened by a slim, black-haired woman of around fifty. She looked just as elegant as her house. "Yes?" she asked.

Andrew Coombs introduced himself as Andi and the others followed him up the steps. The reporter stayed in the driveway, writing something in a small notebook.

"Hmm," said the woman. "I thought I recognized you, Mr. Coombs. I'm Allison Hamilton. Come in." She glanced at Andi and the others with surprise. "A little strange, bringing children along with a vicious snake on the loose, isn't it?"

"Emerald's not vicious," Tristan tried saying, but Ms. Hamilton had disappeared inside with Mr. Coombs.

"I guess we can go in, too," said Natalie. "Right?"

Ms. Hamilton waved them all to take a seat in the enormous kitchen at the back of the house. "I can't tell you any more than I already told the police yesterday afternoon," she said. "Can't you get my statement from them?"

"We'd rather hear it from you, Ms. Hamilton." Andrew Coombs sat on a long wicker couch near a window. Unsure of whether to sit down as well, Andi and the others hovered by the enormous steel refrigerator.

Ms. Hamilton seated herself on the couch beside Andrew. "I saw it on my porch around three o'clock yesterday. Then I came inside, bolted all the doors and windows, and called the police. It was all over in a matter of seconds."

James Henry put his head around the kitchen door. "Mind if we come in as well, Ms. Hamilton?" he asked. "I have to say, you have the most elegant home."

Andi waited for the woman to send the reporter packing. To her surprise, Ms. Hamilton called him inside. "Please join us, James," she said, with the first smile Andi had seen.

Ms. Hamilton obviously knew the sleazy reporter! Andi was astonished.

Tristan spoke up. "What time did you see the snake, Ms. Hamilton?"

Ms. Hamilton frowned, as if she'd forgotten that the Pet Finders were there. "What on earth does a group of children want to know that for?" she asked.

Feeling a little bolder, Andi pulled a Pet Finders Club card she'd made on her computer out of her pocket and walked across to the couch. "We find animals," she explained.

Allison Hamilton rolled her eyes. "This isn't a gerbil we're talking about, my dear."

"Perhaps you read about animals disappearing from a local pet store a couple months back?" Mr. Coombs said. "These kids found them and returned them to the store owner. *Including* a number of reptiles."

James Henry whistled and scribbled something on his notepad.

Andi was pleased to see Ms. Hamilton's expression change from irritation to surprise. "Have a seat, children."

Andi sat down gingerly on the creamy cushions, wondering if her jeans were dirty. Natalie looked totally comfortable, and Andi remembered that Nat's mother and stepfather lived in a house almost as grand as this. Tristan and Simon, meanwhile, hovered about three inches above the cushions as if they were afraid to sit down at all.

"I've heard of you before," Ms. Hamilton was saying to Mr. Coombs. "I'm on a number of museum committees and I've recently put a lot of work into our campaign for better staffing. I can't say I was surprised to hear that it was a staff error that allowed the snake to escape in the first place. What can you expect when there are so few of you?"

"We are understaffed," Mr. Coombs admitted. "But we have an application in for further funding—"

"I couldn't believe it when I heard of the museum's plans to exhibit a number of dangerous animals," Ms. Hamilton interrupted him. "It was only a matter of time before there was a serious incident like this. The museum will need a thorough review of its security."

"Excuse me, Ms. Hamilton?" Tristan put in. "Can you describe the snake?"

"Describe it?" Ms. Hamilton repeated. "It was a snake. What more is there to say?"

"What color was it?" Tristan pressed.

"*Snake*-colored," Ms. Hamilton replied. "It inched

across my front porch like it had all the time in the world. Horrible thing!"

"You said you only saw it for a second," Andi put in. "Are you sure it was a snake?"

"Of course I'm sure!" The woman looked offended. "Snakes are all dangerous creatures, and an understaffed place like the Science Museum has no business exhibiting them. You should concentrate on finding it and stopping it from attacking innocent people, instead of coming around here and asking useless questions. Now, if you'll excuse me, I have a great deal of work to do. I have a meeting with the mayor about museum security in an hour. In light of recent events, it should be a very interesting meeting."

"This latest campaign of yours will really touch our viewers, Ms. Hamilton," James Henry jumped in smoothly. "Could you spare the time for an interview?"

"I can't believe she kicked us out, but let that creep stay and interview her!" Tristan fumed all the way down Earl Drive.

"It's clear she didn't know anything about snakes," Simon added. "Emerald would no more attack someone than stand on her tail and dance a rumba."

Andi was deep in thought. The way Allison Hamilton had complained about museum security—the way she had a meeting lined up with the mayor . . . On top of everything else, Ms. Hamilton had behaved pretty weirdly *and* had James Henry in the palm of her hand. What if she was paying him to write scare stories about the museum? What if . . .

"I know this sounds crazy," Andi ventured, "but is it possible that Ms. Hamilton might be trying to close the museum down?"

Mr. Coombs looked astonished. "But she told us she's on a number of museum committees. I haven't met her before, but I don't have much to do with behind-the-scenes administration. Even if she doesn't like snakes, it's not a crime, Andi!"

"Maybe not," said Andi darkly. "But Ms. Hamilton's up to something. And I'm going to find out what!"

Chapter Ten

Back in the Saunders' kitchen early that afternoon, Andi, Natalie, Tristan, and Simon pored over Tristan's map of Orchard Park they had spread out on the kitchen table.

"The lunchtime news mentioned two more sightings of Emerald," Tristan said. "Here, at Monarch Way and Duke Avenue again." He added two more red circles on the map.

They all stared at the pattern that was starting to emerge.

"The sightings seem to go around in a circle," Simon pointed out.

Andi looked closer. "And Earl Drive's right at the center!" she exclaimed. "That's where Ms. Hamilton lives!"

"Maybe Ms. Hamilton was telling the truth about seeing Emerald after all," Natalie suggested.

"I don't know about that," Andi said. She didn't want

to give up her theory about Ms. Hamilton and her motives for shutting down the museum.

"Well, she said she saw Emerald on her porch," Simon said. "That would match up with snake behavior in cold weather."

Andi was confused. "It would?"

"The porch is made out of wood — and wood is warmer than stone . . . or snow," Tristan explained. "Remember, snakes are cold-blooded. If you were a snake trying to keep warm in the snow and you saw a nice bit of wood to sit on for a while, wouldn't you sit there?"

"I guess so," said Andi doubtfully.

"Also," Simon added with one finger up in the air, "Ms. Hamilton said the snake was moving 'like it had all the time in the world.' Cold snakes don't move very fast, Andi. It does fit."

"Maybe you're right," Andi said with a gulp. She couldn't believe how close she had come to writing off a good clue just because she hadn't liked the witness. "Let's go see her again and try to get some more details about Emerald this time."

Tristan tapped the map thoughtfully. "We need some more information first," he said. "I think Emerald probably has a central safe point in the middle of all this, someplace that's warm enough for a boa to nest and keep out of the snow. Emerald wouldn't have stayed on Ms. Hamilton's porch for long—it's too exposed. We need more information about the area."

"What area's that?" Tristan's older brother Dean sauntered into the kitchen and helped himself to an apple. Crunching into it, he looked over Tristan's shoulder at the map.

"Here." Tristan pointed out Earl Drive and the surrounding blocks.

"Why don't you ask Mom or Dad?" Dean suggested. He finished his apple in four bites, tossing the core in the trash. "That's their favorite part of town. They make more commission on one of those places than they would on the rest of Orchard Park put together."

"Perfect," Andi breathed. "Come on, Tris. Let's go ask them!"

At the Saunders's real estate office on Main Street, the Pet Finders hit gold.

"Here's one we sold a month back," said Mr. Saunders, pulling a glossy brochure from the filing cabinet. "It's Prince Street. Any good?"

Andi glanced at the framed map on the wall. There had been a sighting on Prince Street, she remembered—and it looked like it backed onto Earl Drive. It was a good place to start. "Thanks, Mr. Saunders," she said, taking the details down.

"Plenty of trees," Natalie commented, studying the flyer. "What's this here, in the middle?"

"Looks like a rock garden," Andi said. She frowned. Why did it suddenly seem familiar?

"I remember that place," Mrs. Saunders said, looking over Andi's shoulder. "It had a floodlit pond with this terrific little waterfall. As soon as the client saw it, he had to have it. His name was Mr. Clayton, I think."

"Let me see that!" Tristan snatched the brochure from Andi's hands and studied it. "Boas wouldn't normally seek out water," he said in excitement, "but these rocks look just like the ones in Emerald's enclosure!"

"I thought I'd seen it somewhere before!" Andi exclaimed. Things were starting to make sense now. "Do you think Emerald might have made her nest in there?"

"Could be." Tristan turned and looked at his father. "Dad, you couldn't give us a ride to Prince Street, could you?"

"It's your lucky day," said Mr. Saunders, reaching for his coat. "I'm heading to a showing on Earl Drive in a half hour."

The afternoon light was beginning to fade by the time Mr. Saunders dropped them on Prince Street. The brochure was tucked safely into Andi's pocket. She pulled it out and checked the address.

"Number eleven thirty-eight," she told the others, glancing up at the row of houses in front of them. "It's that modern one over there."

The house had tall windows and was built with white stucco, which was so bright it made the snow look grubby.

"It looks weird—like a spaceship," Natalie said, frowning.

"Cool," Tristan breathed.

They went up the steps and knocked on the gigantic cedar door.

"Yes?" A thin, freckle-faced man in a black turtleneck stood in the doorway.

"Uh, hi," Tristan said and introduced them. "I guess you've heard about the snake that has escaped from the museum?"

"Sure," said the man. "Everyone's talking about it. Is it really as dangerous as they say?"

"Oh, no," Simon reassured him. "That's all hype. But we wondered if we could take a look around your backyard."

The man's sandy-colored eyebrows shot upward. "You think it's in my yard?" To Andi's relief, he grinned.

"If you find it, I'll have a great story to tell in the office tomorrow. Go ahead."

Mr. Clayton showed them through the house.

"It's nice to have a bit of cooperation after Ms. Hamilton, isn't it?" Tristan whispered to Andi and Natalie as they followed Mr. Clayton down the well-lit marble hall, through a bare, space-age kitchen of black marble, and out a set of folding doors to the gravel-covered yard.

Simon stopped in the middle of the rock garden and looked around. "Okay, let's make sure we look in all the crevices," he said. "Boas hate to sit on ice or snow for any length of time."

They searched the rock garden. Andi found that she was holding her breath every time she bent down to peer beneath a likely looking boulder. Much as she wanted to find Emerald, she wasn't too sure about coming face-to-face with a real live boa constrictor. Natalie, she noticed, stayed very close to Tristan and tried not to get too near the rocks.

"Any luck?" Mr. Clayton came down into the yard with a tray in his hands.

"Not yet," Andi began. Suddenly, she heard a familiar voice.

"Still looking for that awful snake? Really, this is getting ridiculous. You should have caught it and destroyed it by now."

Looking around, she saw Allison Hamilton peering over the fence at the back of the garden.

"Yes, we're still looking, Ms. Hamilton," Andi said as politely as she could.

"I didn't know you'd seen it, Cal." Ms. Hamilton looked up at Mr. Clayton.

"I didn't." Mr. Clayton set the tray down on a large rock, and Andi smelled the delicious aroma of hot chocolate wafting from a set of cups. "These kids think it's nesting in my yard, though."

Allison Hamilton turned pale, and Andi realized she was genuinely frightened. "It's just an idea," she said as quickly. She didn't want to upset Ms. Hamilton into calling the police and the press again.

"Are you sure you know what you're doing?" Allison Hamilton looked around a little helplessly. "Aren't there any adults with you? That Mr. Coombs, for example—he's a trained handler, isn't he?"

"Sorry to butt in, Ms. Hamilton," said Natalie brightly, "but is your suit by Paul Mack? He's just my favorite designer. So chic!"

"I . . ." Allison Hamilton focused on Natalie, who was

standing at the fence and smiling at her. "Well, yes—it is," she said at last. "Clever of you to know, my dear. Not many ten-year-olds would notice. I bought it just last spring. . . ."

As Natalie kept Allison Hamilton busy talking about fashion, Andi reached for a steaming cup of hot chocolate and thought about where Emerald might be hiding. Which was the warmest spot in the rock garden?

"Sugar's in the blue pot," Mr. Clayton said, handing Andi a teaspoon.

"Thanks for this, Mr. Clayton," Andi smiled, reaching for the teaspoon. It slipped out of her fingers and fell between two rocks by her feet. "Oh...!" She bent down and tried to spot the teaspoon.

"Look out for the floodlights down there," Mr. Clayton cautioned. "I burned myself on one last summer. But you should be okay—they haven't been on for a few hours."

Tristan swung around. "Floodlights?" he asked. "The brochure did mention floodlights, now that I think about it. How many do you have, Mr. Clayton?"

Andi opened her mouth to ask Tristan why the floodlights were so important—but suddenly realized she knew the answer. *Floodlights would keep the stones warm!* Emerald would have curled up next to them to keep out

of the cold. She wasn't by this one—Andi could see the handle of the teaspoon, but there was no sign of a snake. But she could be close to one of the others. . . .

There were six floodlights around the rock garden. Filled with a burst of determination, Andi searched with Tristan and Simon until they had located them all.

"What about this one, guys?" Andi called, examining a floodlight set close to a cozy-looking crevice at the bottom of the rocks.

Tristan and Simon were both at her side in a moment.

"Emerald's definitely been here," Simon said, trying to control his excitement.

A muddy line moved from the crevice between two rocks, out onto the snowy lawn . . . and through a small gap in Allison Hamilton's fence.

Tristan pointed. "She's left a trail!"

Andi glanced at Ms. Hamilton, who was still chatting to Natalie about some fashion designer she'd never heard of. "How are we going to break the news?" she asked.

"Short, sharp, and to the point," said Tristan cheerfully. "It's usually the best way. Excuse me?" he called. "Ms. Hamilton? I think the missing snake might be on your side of the fence."

Chapter Eleven

Allison Hamilton's face turned pale white as Tristan explained what they'd found. "So you see, Emerald is probably moving through your yard right now," he finished. "Do you think we could come and take a look?"

"I . . . I . . . I . . ." Ms. Hamilton stared in horror at the ground below her feet. "Come through the gate beside that tree," she managed at last. "It links my garden with Mr. Clayton's. I . . . I just need to make a quick phone call. . . ." She rushed across her snowy yard.

"It must be awful to be so afraid of something," Andi commented. They all thanked Mr. Clayton for his time and the hot chocolate, then unlatched the gate.

"Especially something as fantastic as snakes," Simon agreed. "Careful where you're stepping, Natalie—you might rub the trail out with your feet. Look, it heads that way."

The trail wandered across the wide expanse of Ms. Hamilton's lawn, a dark line against the whiteness of the snow. It led to a flowerbed filled with dark green shrubs.

Andi walked slowly across to the flowerbed. Trying not to make any sudden movements that might scare Emerald, she peered between the branches. There was a flash—a dart of reddish brown coils—

"Over here!" she whispered to the others. "She's in here, but she's on the move!" She broke into a jog as she ran alongside the bank of shrubbery, trying not to lose sight of the snake. "She's heading across the yard, toward the house!"

They all ran as fast as they could to the far end of the shrubs. Panting, Simon parted the branches.

"Ew!" Natalie squealed as Emerald slid smoothly out from beneath the branches and slithered across the back porch, which was free of snow. Emerald's pale tan body blended so well with the pale wooden deck that, if it hadn't been for her red markings, they wouldn't have been able to see her at all. Andi watched with horror as the snake slid toward the open end of a pipe—which jutted out from the wall—and disappeared inside the house!

"The front door—quick!" Tristan ordered.

They rang Allison Hamilton's front doorbell. Andi's heart felt as if it was going to leap out of her chest.

Ms. Hamilton opened the door a crack. "Have you found it?" she asked, her voice trembling.

"Kind of," Tristan said breathlessly. "She's just crawled into an open pipe at the back of your house."

Ms. Hamilton gasped.

"Do you know the pipe we mean?" Andi asked, trying to stay calm. "It ends just by your shrubs."

"That's the dryer ventilation pipe," Ms. Hamilton whispered. "It leads to the laundry room. But there's no dryer attached right now. I'm getting a new one."

"Let's go," Tristan said, and Ms. Hamilton let them inside.

The laundry room was warm and detergent-scented and located just off the kitchen. A basket of freshly pressed towels and sheets lay on the floor beside the mouth of the ventilation pipe. And lying on top of a snowy white towel, right in the middle of the basket, lay Emerald.

"Found you, my beauty," Simon murmured, gazing at Emerald's strong, beautifully marked body.

"Looks like she's waiting for a snake charmer to lure

her out of the basket," Andi joked. She turned to Natalie, who was hovering at the door. "Nat, call Mr. Coombs at the museum, okay? I'll block off the pipe in case Emerald decides to make a break for it."

Emerald didn't look as if she was going anywhere. She blinked up at them sleepily from the cozy towels. Andi marveled at her dark eyes, which gleamed like little jewels against her patterned skin.

Allison Hamilton peered through the doorway and stared at the snake in her laundry basket. "She's not leaving slime marks on my towels, I hope," she said.

"Snakes aren't slimy," Tristan assured her. "They're actually very smooth and dry to touch."

The woman leaned in a little. "She's . . . actually quite pretty, isn't she?"

"Don't worry, Ms. Hamilton," Natalie said, snapping her cell phone shut. "Mr. Coombs will be here in a flash. He'll box up Emerald and whisk her back to the museum, where she belongs. You'll never have to see her again."

Andi was amazed to see something like disappointment in Ms. Hamilton's eyes.

On Friday morning, Andi opened her eyes and smiled sleepily at the ceiling. *Another successful case for the Pet*

Finders Club, she thought, remembering how Andrew Coombs had arrived at Ms. Hamilton's house. Tristan and Simon had helped to load the sleepy Emerald into a special carrying case. Ms. Hamilton had stayed close throughout the operation, even asking a few questions about Emerald's markings and her natural habitat.

On Andi's bedside table, her cell phone started ringing. It was Mrs. O'Connor.

"You do know that Mr. Forster is bringing his gelding to Hollow Creek this afternoon at three o'clock, don't you, Andi?" she asked, sounding worried. "What do you plan to do with Perdita?"

All Andi's warm feelings of success suddenly disappeared. She felt sick. Was it really Friday already? How could she have forgotten about Perdita?

"We don't know what to do," she said desperately. "We've tried everything, Mrs. O'Connor—animal shelters, adoption agencies, ranches. Please, *please* can't Perdita stay with you for a little longer? In the barn, maybe? Or—or in that shelter by the paddock? I know it's kind of drafty, but at least it's a roof, and—"

"You know I'd say yes, if I had the space." Mrs. O'Connor sounded sad.

Andi could hear Neil's voice in the background.

"Hold on a minute, will you, Andi?" Mrs. O'Connor said after a brief pause. "Neil's trying to tell me something . . ." She covered the receiver to talk to Neil.

There was a scrabbling sound at her door, and Buddy's face peered around the corner. Seeing Andi looking miserable, he leaped onto the bed and started licking her hands.

"Are you still there, Andi?" It was Neil's voice this time.

Andi pressed the receiver close to her ear. "Give me some good news, will you, Neil?" she begged. "Right now, I really need it."

"Well, how's this?" Neil said. "There's an estate sale at Mrs. Osmond's place at ten o'clock this morning. You know, the old lady whose ponies were in the trailer accident? I just saw the ad in the paper this morning. An estate sale means it's an open house: Anyone can come in and take a look. There's still a whole lot of stuff that the lawyers are selling—furniture and some more livestock, I guess. We should go check it out in case we can find some clues about Perdita!"

Andi felt a surge of hope. She'd never been able to shake the feeling that Perdita had belonged to the old lady, even after Eddie, the auction yard guy, had denied it. Maybe visiting the yard would settle her hunch once and for all.

"I'll be there," she promised, leaping out of bed and scrabbling for something to wear. "I'll call Natalie and Tristan, and we'll meet you there in one hour!"

Natalie's mom offered to drop them off at the stable yard. The address was listed in the ad as Pines Road.

"Pines Road," Andi told the others in excitement as Mrs. Peters drove out of the town and past Hollow Creek. "Do you think it's the same Pines Road where the trailer accident took place?"

"It's the only one I know of," Natalie said, nodding.

Pines Road turned out to be dark and windy and hedged in with forest. Andi peered through the trees, trying to locate old Mr. Clarkwell's cabin. She felt sure that it was somewhere deep in the trees, just out of sight—far enough away from Creek Hollow, but somewhere close to where the accident would have taken place. *We're going to solve this case*, she thought gleefully. *I know we are!*

At last the trees thinned out and Andi could see fenced paddocks and a low ranch-style house on the right, its driveway framed by a pair of large iron gates. The gates were wide open, and a sign beside them read ESTATE SALE TODAY, 10 A.M.

Mrs. Peters carefully negotiated the ruts and patches

of ice that glimmered on the driveway, turning in to park beside a row of other cars. There were a number of people around, some carrying notebooks, others talking on cell phones. Ducks and chickens scattered, squawking, as Andi and the others climbed out of the car and looked around.

Andi spotted Neil and his mom and headed over to them. "Ducks!" she exclaimed, as several glossy-feathered birds darted around her feet.

"Same to you," Neil said humorously.

"No, *ducks*," Andi insisted. "Perdita loves your ducks, doesn't she? Maybe she got used to them when she was living here."

"So?" Tristan pointed out, as he and Natalie joined them. "It's hardly the only place in Seattle with ducks."

Andi shook her head impatiently. "I've just got a hunch, okay? Let's go find a stable hand and see if he remembers Perdita."

But once again, the Pet Finders were out of luck. "None of the original staff work here anymore," a balding man in the estate office told them. "When Mrs. Osmond died, we had to let them go."

"That guy must be one of Mrs. Osmond's lawyers!" Tristan hissed at Andi. "Quick, let's ask him if he knows whether Mrs. Osmond had a gray mare."

But before Andi managed to ask the question, the phone on the estate desk started ringing. Shrugging apologetically, the lawyer answered it.

"Let's take a look around while he's busy," Neil suggested as they stepped back out into the yard. "Look, the stables are over there."

Andi counted three stables, side by side. There had been three ponies in the trailer, hadn't there? More circumstantial evidence, she had to admit. She peered over the half-door of the first stable and found it swung open at her touch.

Inside, the stable was cold and dim, and smelled very faintly of horse. Andi touched the plank walls, trying to sense Perdita there. The straw on the ground was old and dry, the water trough and hay net both empty.

Her shoulder banged against something. "Ouch!" Andi examined her shoulder and realized with dismay that something had ripped a jagged line through the fabric of her coat. Running her hand along the stable wall, she discovered a nail head sticking out more than an inch out on the wall.

"In here!" she called to the others. "Look at this!"

Tristan, Natalie, and Neil all peered over the half-door.

"It's a nail," said Tristan. "So what?"

"There was an old scar on Perdita's withers, remember?" Andi said. She showed them the rip in her coat. "It was a similar shape to this—a jagged kind of question mark!"

The others looked blank.

"Don't you see?" Andi pressed on. "This could have been Perdita's stable! She might have torn her shoulder on this exact nail!"

"But it's still not *real* evidence," Neil said. "Until we find something solid that we can connect to Perdita, we can't prove anything."

Andi noticed that Neil looked oddly relieved as he said this.

"You don't want to find Perdita's owner, do you, Neil?" she said, realizing.

Neil looked guilty. "What do you mean? Of course I do."

Andi tried again. "I mean, you love Perdita now and you don't want to see her go."

"I do love her," Neil admitted, scuffing the ground with the toe of his boot. "But that doesn't mean I don't want to find her owner. I want what's best for her, that's all."

"What's best for her is staying with you at Hollow Creek," Natalie said with a sigh. "Anyone can see that."

"That's not an option, I'm afraid," said Mrs. O'Connor,

shaking her head. "We've only got four hours until Mr. Forster arrives with Puffin."

Andi summoned every ounce of hope that things would work out. "Everything's going to be fine," she said with determination, squeezing Neil's arm encouragingly. "You'll see."

But unfortunately when they went to look for the lawyer for the Osmond estate, they couldn't find him. He was no longer on the phone, and although they hunted everywhere, there was no sign of the balding man who might have been able to answer their one, all-important question: Had Perdita belonged to Mrs. Osmond or not?

"We can't wait around any longer," Mrs. O'Connor advised, checking her watch. "It's past eleven, and I've got a student at noon for an hour. Plus we've got work to do, getting Puffin's stable ready. Andi, you really have to call your ASPCA friend again and ask about housing Perdita tonight."

"Let's go back to the auction yard," Andi begged, desperate not to give up just yet. "We've got to talk to that Eddie guy again."

"I can't see him changing his story unless we get some more evidence." Natalie sighed. "Look, I've still got that picture of Perdita on my cell phone. Maybe if we show it to him, he'll remember her."

"We found Emerald, so we can find Perdita's owner," Tristan declared. "There's just one missing link that will tie everything together, I'm sure of it."

Andi was sure that Tristan was right. But how would they find the link?

Chapter Twelve

After much persuasion, Mrs. O'Connor agreed to drive the kids over to McVitie's Auction House at one o'clock that afternoon, after her lesson. Meanwhile, they headed back to Hollow Creek, where they faced the task of having to move Perdita from her stable into the barn.

"Is there any way at all that Perdita can stay in the barn tonight?" Andi pleaded as Mrs. O'Connor led the gray mare across the yard. Tristan, Neil, and Natalie followed close behind.

Mrs. O'Connor stopped and looked at Andi. "It's not the solution, though, is it?" she said gently. "The same problem will be here tomorrow, and the day after, and the day after that. Isn't it time we passed responsibility for Perdita over to an adoption agency?"

Andi leaned her head against Perdita's warm cheek for a moment. "Okay," she said, fighting back the tears.

"But only if we don't get answers at the auction house. Agreed?"

Mrs. O'Connor smiled. "Agreed." She patted Perdita's flank. "She's a lovely girl. If I could keep her, I would."

They put Perdita in a corner of the barn and set to work cleaning out her stable for the new arrival. Then the kids had a quick bite to eat and started to clean up the tack room, to pass the time while Mrs. O'Connor worked with her riding student in the sand school. It was very cozy, thanks to a large heater working overtime in the corner.

Andi threw herself into the task of shining up the tack, working the polish into the warm leather. Natalie helped Neil sort out blankets for washing and mending, while Tristan washed a selection of headcollars in a bucket of warm, soapy water. Andi realized how much she would miss Hollow Creek when they had to go back to school on Monday.

"Hey!" Tristan held up Perdita's familiar-looking blue headcollar. "This has been fixed recently."

"Mrs. O'Connor must have taken it to get fixed this week," said Andi, not looking up from the saddle she was polishing.

"No," Tristan insisted. He thrust the headcollar under Andi's nose. "That part's still broken. I mean an *earlier* mending. Look here—there's different stitching around the headband."

Andi took the headcollar and looked closely at it. Thin white stitching had been worked into a break in the thick blue webbing. It looked fairly new, judging from the whiteness of the thread. How had they missed it before? It was another clue! Maybe if they found who mended it, they could get a lead on Perdita's owner.

Mrs. O'Connor gave them a list of four local saddlers who mended headcollars. "I'm taking those rugs to Malley's to get them fixed this morning," she said, nodding at the pile of old blankets Natalie and Neil had been sorting out. "You can come along if you want. It's a good place to start looking."

Malley's turned out to be a rambling place, filled to the brim with piles of new fleecy horse rugs, boxes of bits and bridle rings, racks of jodhpurs and riding boots and velvet-colored helmets.

"This wasn't done by us," said the man behind the counter, turning the headcollar around in his hands. "Have you tried Mr. Agnelli yet?"

Andi checked her list of saddlers. The name "Agnelli" wasn't on there.

"He's retired now," the storeowner explained, leaning his elbows on the counter. "But he still takes in a bit of work." He studied the neat white stitching again. "Yes, looks very much like Agnelli," he said, nodding. "You'll find him just a couple of blocks from here."

"Wouldn't it be awesome if Mr. Agnelli fixed the head-collar? He could tell us where it came from and we'll finally solve the case!" Andi said excitedly, after they had explained this latest twist to Mrs. O'Connor. Then the kids headed out in search of Mr. Agnelli's workshop.

"Don't get your hopes up," Tristan warned as they walked down the street. "It could be another false lead."

Andi stopped outside an old building with a faded sign in the window that read Agnelli's. "It can't be," she said with determination, and pushed open the door. "I mean, how many red herrings can one pony leave?"

Andi was right. This time, they struck pure gold.

"I remember it well," said Mr. Agnelli, a portly man with a shock of white hair that stood on end like a parrot's crest. He studied the headcollar and looked up. "Mrs. Osmond was a good customer for years before I retired. She wouldn't trust anyone but Agnelli with a job like this." He smiled in satisfaction, admiring his handi-work. "This was for her favorite pony—a gray mare, as I remember. She was a beauty."

Andi could have kissed him. Mrs. Osmond owned a

gray mare! The proof they'd been looking for! She felt like cartwheeling through the man's dusty old workshop. "That's awesome, Mr. Agnelli," she said. "It means that we've just solved our case! Our gray mare belonged to Mrs. Osmond all along!"

She glanced happily at the others. Tristan was grinning, too, but Neil and Natalie were both looking at the floor. Andi's good mood wilted as she realized what this meant. Perdita would be auctioned on behalf of Mrs. Osmond's estate—and would have to leave Hollow Creek. They might never see her again.

As they left Mr. Agnelli's workshop, Andi tried her best to comfort Neil. "Maybe you could buy her," she said. "I mean, your mom is always looking for new ponies, right?"

Neil shrugged. "We probably can't afford her," he said. "Plus, there's no room for her in the yard. Maybe it's for the best that she's sold to someone else."

"It seems like she belongs at Hollow Creek!" said Nat.

They had reached the gates of McVitie's Auction House. Andi squared her shoulders and marched into the yard. It was time to find Eddie, the guy who had been cleaning out the auction ring. He couldn't deny Perdita had been in the trailer now, could he? Andi wanted to know why he'd tried to throw them off the trail.

This time Eddie wasn't alone in the ring. A man with a thin ponytail and a stomach that hung low over the waistband of his jeans stood with him.

"Back again?" Eddie asked, recognizing them. "I told you all I know."

"We brought a picture this time," Andi said as Natalie took out her phone. "Would you mind taking a look?"

"What's this about, Ed?" asked the man.

"That trailer accident you had, Tom," Eddie replied. Andi realized with a sudden flash of interest that this must be the driver, back from his vacation.

Natalie held out the phone to Tom and Eddie.

"Sure we know this pony," said the driver, scratching his large stomach. "She was the pretty one. Did we ever catch her, Eddie?"

Eddie studied the photo. "Don't think we did," he said.

Andi pounced. "You said there were no grays in the trailer on the day of the accident! How come?"

Eddie looked at her as if she was nuts. "This pony's *not* gray! It's white."

Tom jabbed Eddie in the ribs. "White horses are called grays."

"Huh? Then what are gray ones called?" Eddie asked in confusion.

"Darned if I know," Tom said cheerfully. He turned to Andi. "That answer your question?"

It did, Andi reflected, as the final piece of the puzzle fell into place. *It most certainly did.*

Mrs. O'Connor came hurrying across the auction yard. Her face looked strangely lit up, and she was holding her cell phone high in the air.

"We've proven that Perdita belonged to Mrs. Osmond," Andi began. "If we head back to the estate sale, we can find the lawyer and arrange for Perdita to stay in her old stable tonight. I told you it would work out okay! We—"

"I've got something else to tell you!" Mrs. O'Connor interrupted, laughing. "You won't believe it, but Mr. Forster just canceled his booking for Puffin. It looks like Perdita can stay at Hollow Creek after all!"

"Yes!" Andi cried, slapping a round of high fives to her friends. Now Perdita would be safe and warm tonight—and every night until the beautiful gray mare found a loving new home.

"All this waiting around is making me nervous," Natalie complained a week later as the Pet Finders gathered together in the yard a Hollow Creek.

"Making *you* nervous?" Andi echoed. "What about Neil and his mom?"

"If it affects Neil, it affects Nat," said Tristan sarcastically—and was rewarded with a punch on the arm from Natalie.

Andi leaned over Perdita's stable door. The snowy-white mare whickered softly and nodded her head at Andi, who tried to stroke the mare's nose. She never tired of feeling Perdita's sleek coat beneath her fingers.

"The call should have come from the auction house by now," Natalie said. "Do you think this means the O'Connors didn't bid enough?"

"Don't be so gloomy!" Andi exclaimed. "Maybe the bidding is still going on . . ." She trailed off. There was no way that Mrs. O'Connor would be on the phone, today of all days—not with Perdita's auction taking place.

"This'll cheer you up." Tristan pulled a folded newspaper out of his coat pocket and handed it to Andi.

"'*The Rain Forest Exhibition at the Science Museum closed today, after record attendance numbers,*'" Andi read. "'*This was due in no small part to the dramatic escape two weeks ago of Emerald, a rare South American boa constrictor, and her equally dramatic rescue. "Exhibitions like these are essential for our children's education," said Ms. Allison Hamilton, spokeswoman for the Friends of the Science Museum. "I learned a great deal about the wild creatures of the rain forests and have put my own phobia of snakes behind me. The museum has the whole-hearted support of my organization, and we hope they continue to raise awareness in the future with more eye-opening exhibitions like this."'"*

The office door swung open. Andi and the others swung around to see swung tearing across the yard toward them. "We got her!" he yelled. "We got Perdita!"

Andi got lost in a sea of hugs—from Neil and Tristan and Natalie. Even Buddy and Jet tried to join in, jumping around and barking with delight. Perdita put her head casually over her stable door.

"Don't you mean Snowstorm?" Andi corrected, laughing as she pulled herself out of the tangle of arms. They had finally learned the gray mare's name from papers held by the auction house.

Neil grinned. "Mrs. Osmond gave her a terrific name, but she'll always be Perdita to us." He dropped a kiss on Perdita's velvety nose. "You're all ours now, 'lost one,'" he said softly.

Andi raised a finger. "You know, she was never really lost," she corrected him, smiling. "It looks like she was home all along!"

About the Author

Ben Baglio was born in New York, and grew up in a small town in southern New Jersey. He was the only boy in a family with three sisters.

Ben spent a lot of his childhood reading. English was always his favorite subject, and after graduating from high school, he went on to study English Literature at the University of Pennsylvania. During his coursework, he was able to spend a year in Edinburgh, Scotland.

After graduation, Ben Baglio worked as a children's book editor in New York City. He also wrote his first book, which was about the Olympics in ancient Greece. Five years later, he took a job at a publishing house in England.

Ben Baglio is the author of the *Dolphin Diaries* series, and is perhaps most well known for the *Animal Ark* and *Animal Ark Hauntings* series. These books were originally published in England (under the pseudonym Lucy Daniels), and have since gone on to be published in the United States and translated into 15 languages.

Aside from writing, Ben enjoys scuba diving and swimming, music and movies. He has a beagle named Bob, who is by his side whenever he writes.